W.J. Burley lives with ~~~~~ Newquay, and is a Corn~~~~~ back five generations. He started life as an engineer, and later went to Balliol to read zoology as a mature student. On leaving Oxford he went into teaching and, until his retirement, was a senior biology master in a large mixed grammar school in Newquay. He created Inspector (now Chief Superintendent) Wycliffe in 1966, and has featured him in Cornish detective novels ever since, the series has recently been televised with Jack Shepherd starring in the title role.

WYCLIFFE AND THE QUIET VIRGIN

W. J. Burley

CORGI BOOKS

Mulfra is a tiny hamlet in Penwith, known for its chamber tomb or 'quoit'. I have taken the liberty of using the name for a village on the coast road between Zennor and Morvah, a village which only exists in the pages of this book.

W.J.B.

WYCLIFFE AND THE QUIET VIRGIN
A CORGI BOOK: 0 552 13435 X

Originally published in Great Britain by
Victor Gollancz Ltd.

PRINTING HISTORY
Victor Gollancz edition published 1986
Corgi edition published 1989
Corgi edition reprinted 1991
Corgi edition reprinted 1994
Corgi edition reprinted 1997

This book is set in Baskerville 10/11pt by
Chippendale Type, Otley, West Yorkshire

Corgi Books published by Transworld Publishers Ltd.,
61-63 Uxbridge Road, London W5 5SA,
in Australia by Transworld Publishers (Australia) Pty, Ltd.,
15-25 Helles Avenue, Moorebank, NSW 2170,
and in New Zealand by Transworld Publishers (N.Z.) Ltd.,
3 William Pickering Drive, Albany, Auckland.

Printed and bound in Great Britain by
Mackays of Chatham PLC, Chatham, Kent

CHAPTER ONE

Marsden opened his eyes; the plaster between the rafters was greyish white, the rafters themselves cobalt blue, painted by Emma; spiders' webs in the corners. The light from the little window was grey and cold, the air damp; even the sheets felt clammy. He could hear Emma downstairs in the kitchen, running water, the only place in the house where there was water and that came from an overhead tank, pumped from a well.

Marsden scratched himself.

Twenty-five minutes to nine by the alarm clock on the little cast-iron mantelpiece which was also cobalt blue. Marsden raised himself on his elbow so that he could see out of the window. Fine rain out of a leaden sky.

'Bloody hell!'

The front door slammed, then the car door; the starter of Emma's M-registered Mini whined a couple of times, seemed to give up, then in its last gasp, set the little engine puttering. An uncertain cough or two, a spluttering in the exhaust, and Emma was away.

Marsden got out of bed; a large man, fleshy without being fat, powerful; built like a gorilla. A mop of black hair, and a generous moustache; good features, eyes wide apart, and a broad, high forehead. He thought he looked like Balzac and cultivated the resemblance. The locals said that he had Romany blood and that pleased him too. He was forty-six.

He stood by the window, stooping to clear the sloping roof. Down the narrow valley mist blotted out the sea. Brown smoke came from the Lemarques' chimney, the only house he could see, perched some way up the opposite hill, white against the sludge-green heather. A mail van picked a cautious way along the old mine track which led there. He pulled on a paint-stained dressing-gown, fished his slippers from under the bed with his toes, and wriggled his feet into them without stooping. He slouched across the room to the landing, the floorboards creaked under his weight and the jars and bottles on Emma's dressing table clinked together. He negotiated the narrow, twisted stairs down to the living-room.

A large, square table covered with a plastic cloth and on it, a battered blue enamelled coffee pot and a mug inscribed 'Hugh' (from the days when Emma still believed that he could be domesticated). There was a note in Emma's writing propped against the milk jug: 'I've shut that blasted cat out because he messed in the kitchen again. If it's still there when I come home this evening you'll be doing the cooking, not me.'

'Bitch!' Mechanical, without venom.

Marsden opened the front door; the cat, a complacent tabby, was asleep in the shelter of the porch. Marsden picked him up, made soothing noises, and carried him indoors. He poured milk into a saucer and put it on the floor. 'There, Percy, old boy! She's gone now.' The cat lapped up the milk, purring away like a Rolls Royce.

Marsden felt the coffee pot then went to the kitchen to warm it on the stove. While he was in the kitchen he splashed cold water over his face and groped for the towel. The flow from the tap was a mere trickle. 'The bloody tank's empty again!'

With his mug full of black coffee he came back through the living-room and into his studio, followed by the cat. The studio was a lean-to built on to the end of the house in times past, as stabling for mules. With his own hands he had removed the roof and replaced it with corrugated perspex which gave a diffused north light when it was not covered with moss and gull shit.

6

He ferreted about, looking for matches, and when he found them he lit the paraffin stove. There was an electric heater but he used that only when he had a model. A canvas stood on one of the two easels: a landscape, blocked in. Although Marsden was best known for his landscapes and marines he was a studio painter. 'None of that muffler and hot-water bottle crap for me; I find my *plein air* in the studio next to the oil-stove; "Emotion recollected in tranquility" – in comfort anyway.' He reached for a brush from the pot, changed his mind and drank his coffee instead, in two or three great gulps. Then he lit a cigarette. Marsden was coming to life, the skin round his eyes seemed less taut and his mouth had lost its sour taste. He moved to the second easel where there was another canvas, this one covered by a cloth; he removed the cloth and stood looking at the painting: Portrait of a Young Girl. She wore a flowered wrap which had slipped to expose one breast, and she regarded herself in a large mirror with an ornately carved frame; her expression intent, frowning. Red-gold hair reached to her shoulders, her cheeks were lightly flushed. Marsden had caught the fine delicacy of the girl's brows, of her lashes, of her lips but mostly he had captured her total self-absorption.

He stood back. 'Marsden, my boy, you're a painter!'

The mirror and the padded seat were still set up in one corner of the studio.

He had told Emma nothing of the sittings which had taken place while she was at work and his studio was sacrosanct, but yesterday he had shown her the painting. He could have written the script in advance:

'That's the Lemarque girl.'

'Full marks for observation.'

'She's jail-bait in any language. How did you manage it? At that age they want more than sweeties. Really, Hugh, you must be out of your mind!'

'I painted the girl, I didn't screw her.'

'Even if I believed you it wouldn't make any difference; she's quite capable of saying that you did.'

'If it came to that I'd prefer her mother; there's a dark little mystery package that needs working on! Unfortunately, now that her husband's out of clink, there's a sitting tenant.'

'You're vile!'

His palette for the painting, covered with cling-film, stood on a table by the easel. He couldn't make up his mind whether or not he had finished with it. He replaced the cloth and started to sing in a croaking baritone: 'The rich get richer and the poor get children'.

The cat, couchant by the oil-stove, tucked in his paws and prepared for sleep.

Marsden said: 'I wonder what she would do if somebody locked her in without a loo,' and chuckled at the thought. 'I tell you what, Percy, I'll make you a cat-flap. I know I've said it before but this time I really will!'

The letter-box in the front door rattled and he went back to the living-room.

A small shower of mail on the mat. Marsden gathered it up and shuffled through the envelopes with a certain urgency, then he seemed to relax: Christmas cards for Emma, a couple of circulars, an electricity bill, a letter from a West End gallery: '. . . We regret that we cannot offer you a one-man show in the coming year but if you will consider joining with—' Marsden screwed up the letter and aimed it at the fireplace. 'No, sir! Not with that bloody ponce. We haven't got quite there yet.'

The final envelope was also for Emma. He recognized brother Tim's prissy italic script and he knew those letters by heart as Emma always left them lying about. There would be the usual news of successful-accountant brother Tim, of his pasty-faced wife, and of their two brats – with snapshots thrown in to highlight the attractions of conjugal felicity. Then the brotherly advice: variations on a theme – 'I've heard from mum and dad again. Really, Em, I can't understand why you

8

throw yourself away on that man. Apart from being an absolute scoundrel, he's nearly old enough to be your father . . . '

'I am old enough to be her bloody father,' Marsden had said. 'I started early.' He propped Emma's mail on the mantelpiece, against a vase in the form of a fish standing on its tail.

'He's right though, Marsden, you scum! Give the gentleman his sister back.'

The time had come to allow her family to entice Emma away. She was taking over and, in any case, life had grown too complicated.

He opened the front door to stand in his little porch, looking up at the sky. Fine rain still drizzled out of low cloud. *'Gloom!* Damp, grey, dreary, bloodless gloom!' Eight hours between sunrise and sunset, the twenty-third of December, two days to Christmas, the very nadir of the year.

Jane Lemarque was in her living-room; a smoky fire burned in the grate, the room was furnished with unmatched and incongruous pieces which looked what they were, random discards from a more affluent home. She stood by the window, looking out on a familiar scene; mist hid the sea and inland she could just distinguish the grey rectangular bulk of the church tower. This, and the hill opposite, scarred by old mine-workings and capped by a great cairn of boulders, set the limits of her world for days at a time.

Jane had dark hair and deep blue eyes, an oval face, rather pale; and an expression of madonna-like serenity. Only people who knew her well (and few did) realized that though she might seem passive she was anything but serene. Even now as she stood gazing out of the window her lips moved and she murmured a barely articulate form of words, half prayer, half incantation: 'Please God make it all come right . . . Oh, Lord, don't

9

let it happen . . . Dear Lord I promise . . . Don't let Francine . . . Don't let Alain . . . '

She looked across at the painter's cottage, crouched at the foot of the hill, last of the struggling outliers of the village. Marsden, in his dressing-gown, was standing in his porch, staring up at the sky. The sight of the man increased her disquiet. Recently she had tried to avoid coming face to face with him but sometimes on her way to or from the village they would meet. He was always polite but he looked at her in such an intimate and knowing way that she felt vulnerable, naked, so that her flesh trembled and her face burned.

Now he was taking an interest in Francine, encouraging and helping her with her painting; he had given her colours and brushes which she believed were expensive to buy. 'Please don't let . . . '

Her attention was distracted from the painter by a figure in an anorak trudging along the narrow road which led from the cove, past the painter's cottage and on to the village. Paul Bateman, youngest of the Bishop clan. The Bishops, Penzance lawyers for generations, lived at Mynhager House down by the cove. Paul was seventeen and for the past six months he had pursued Francine with earnest solicitude. Either he was on his way to the village or he was coming to see her now and she was still in bed. Jane watched the boy. He had reached the painter's cottage and he would continue along the road or he would turn off down a steep footpath to the bridge over the stream. Jane watched him. 'Please God he doesn't come here . . . Please God . . .' But God wasn't listening, the boy turned down the footpath to the bridge.

Agitated, Jane went to the bottom of the stairs and called to her daughter. She could hear the radio playing, the eternal Radio One.

'Francine!' She called twice before she was answered by a voice that sounded petulant rather than sleepy.

'What is it?'

'Paul is on his way here.'

Silence.

'It's nearly half-past nine, don't you think it's time you got up?' Pleading.

'Tell him I'm sick.'

'I can't tell him a deliberate lie.'

'Why not? You want to stop me seeing him.'

'I didn't say that, Francine! I said it wouldn't be a good idea to let your friendship with Paul grow into something more. That doesn't mean—'

'I wish you'd make up your mind what you do mean.' But the radio was switched off. 'All right, I'm coming down.'

Jane felt tears of misery and frustration smarting in her eyes. She returned to the window. Paul was climbing the flight of steps which led up to the front door. She opened the door before he knocked but did not invite him in. The boy stood there, long and lean, droplets of moisture dripping from his hair and running down his face.

'I wondered if Francine would come with me to St Ives this afternoon. John Falls is putting on an exhibition of those crazy models of his. He thinks he might sell one or two as Christmas presents and I said I would come.'

'I can't. I've got the play at the church this evening.' Francine had come downstairs silently; she was wearing a track suit, her hair uncombed about her shoulders.

'I know, but we shall go in the car and be back long before then.' Paul had just passed his driving test.

'I've got to finish learning my lines.'

Jane said, 'So Paul has wasted his trip over here. Why didn't you phone, Paul?'

The boy looked embarrassed. 'I didn't mind the walk.' He lingered. 'If Francine can't come this afternoon perhaps I could pick you both up this evening and take you to the church – unless Mr Lemarque is going . . .'

11

Jane felt trapped, she didn't dare refuse. 'That is kind of you, Paul. I don't think he will be going.'

'Half-past seven, then . . . Will that do? Earlier if you want.'

'Half-past seven will be all right,' Francine said.

Paul smiled uncertainly and took himself off.

Jane looked sorrowfully at her daughter. 'Really, Francine!'

'What have I done now?'

At Mynhager House, down by the cove, Virginia Bishop was perched on a tall step-ladder in a corner of the big drawing-room, pinning up the last of the Christmas decorations. Elaborate though faded paper-chains festooned from the central chandelier and there was a Christmas tree, draped with tinsel and hung with shiny balls and coloured lights. Seen from this unfamiliar angle the room seemed more shabby than ever; the colours of wallpaper, upholstery, carpet and curtains had merged to the same drab fawn; the gilt-framed oil paintings might have been hanging in a saleroom and the sprigs of holly tucked behind their frames seemed absurdly incongruous. Even the grand piano, Carrie's pride and joy, had a bluish bloom on its polished lid.

Virginia looked down at her sister, kneeling on the floor, putting away unwanted decorations for another year, putting them back into a box which had held them for a lifetime. Virginia thought: Caroline is putting on weight, and slacks do nothing for her figure. At least I've kept slim. Of course, she drinks too much. There was a time when people used to take us for twins. They couldn't now.

She came down the steps and brushed her hands together. 'That cornice is thick with dust.'

'You say that every year, Vee.'

Virginia stood by the window. 'This damned mist, you can't see a thing.'

'What do you expect in December? If it's not fog it's

12

wind.' Caroline got to her feet and stooped to massage her knees. 'Well, that's done for another year, thank God! Why do we bother? Christmas! I feel worn out already and it hasn't even started.'

'We've got Ernest's friend, Wycliffe, coming this afternoon.'

'I can do without reminding. I wish Ernest wouldn't invite people here to stay. Poor old Ada is getting beyond it and the extra work falls on us.'

'Mother used to cope with a houseful.'

'Mother was a marvel but don't let's start getting all sentimental or I shall howl. I need a drink.'

'Where's Paul?'

'I'm not sure but I think he's gone to see Francine.'

'He's been seeing a lot of her recently.'

'Yes, I'd rather he wasn't.'

'Why?'

'For one thing I think she's got all the makings of a little whore.'

'And?'

'Isn't that enough?'

'Yes, but I don't think it's true. I think we see the worst side of Francine. Jenny Eggerton is her form mistress and she was saying Francine's main trouble is that she keeps herself too much to herself. She holds everybody at arm's length – other girls, staff, and boys. Incidentally, Jenny was at a rehearsal for the vicar's nativity play and she was really impressed by Francine's performance as the Virgin.'

'I don't doubt she puts on a good act but she would need to in that role.'

'She's got a wonderful voice for a girl of her age.'

'I know, but that doesn't stop me wishing she would keep away from Paul. Not that what I think will make any difference; I'm only his mother.' Caroline moved towards the door. 'I'm going to fetch that drink; are you sure you won't have something?'

'All right, a small sherry, just to celebrate.'

Virginia was left alone. Thirty-five, a spinster, a teacher of biology in a comprehensive school; at nineteen it would have seemed a fate worse than death, now she thought there were compensations. The mist had thinned and through the mullioned window she could see the lichen-covered balustrade at the end of the terrace and the grey sea beyond. To her left she glimpsed the hump of Gurnard's Head only to lose it again almost at once. Mynhager House, built on the rock platform of an ancient landslip, facing four-square to the Atlantic and backing on a steep boulder-strewn slope.

'Here we are, then!' Caroline with a whisky and a dry sherry on a tray.

They sat on one of the massive settees.

Virginia said: 'Are you meeting Gerald off the train this evening?'

'No, he's driving down, thank goodness!'

'How long is he down for?'

Caroline sipped her whisky. 'I've no idea. The House reassembles on the seventh or eighth but with luck he should have gone back before then. There's a cabinet reshuffle in the wind and they're all running round in circles with their little pink tongues hanging out. It seems Sir James is almost certain to be kicked upstairs to the Lords and if that happens, Stafford will step into his shoes and Stafford has more than hinted to Gerald that he would be very much in the running as his P.P.S.'

'Gerald will end up in the cabinet himself one of these days.'

Caroline pouted. 'If he doesn't it won't be for the want of keeping in with the right people.'

'You're hard on that husband of yours.'

'You think so?'

'You won't even live in his constituency.'

'I told him when we were married, "This is my home".'

'He wasn't an MP then.'

'That's his affair.' Caroline rolled the whisky tumbler

14

between her plump hands. 'Incidentally, I shall be out this afternoon.'

'Isn't your car in dock? Of course you can borrow mine if you want it.'

'Thanks all the same, but I can walk where I'm going.' Caroline said this with a certain smugness.

Virginia looked at her sister, perplexed at first, then accusing: 'You're going to see Marsden!'

'How did you guess?'

Virginia was shocked; she got up and crossed to the window. 'Really, Carrie! You told me that was all over . . . It's like going to a brothel.'

'Why not? Women's lib and all that. But perhaps you'd prefer it if he came here?' Caroline yawned. 'There's no point in turning pi on me, Vee. For Christ's sake try living in the real world for once!'

'With your son here and your husband coming home tonight . . . I just don't know what to say!'

'Then don't say anything, dear. I need a man now and then, a real man, it's as simple as that. Sleeping with Gerald is like bedding down with a wet fish – and that's all I've got to look forward to for the next week at least. I don't know how you manage and I don't ask; perhaps we're different.'

'My God, I hope so! It's obscene!'

Caroline sounded bored. 'Don't be so damned self-righteous, Vee!'

Two o'clock. Joseph Bishop's glasses had slipped to the end of his nose and his eyes were closed; a long, thin hand rested on the open book in his lap. At seventy-four Joseph remained physically active and mentally alert but in the hour after lunch he was often overtaken by drowsiness which he resented and did his best to combat. He usually took his exercise in the mornings, walking on the cliffs or over the moor, and in the afternoons he read, though now his reading was increasingly restricted to books he had read before.

15

When he drowsed he seemed to be half remembering, half dreaming of the days when his father was alive and Mynhager House was still part of the cultural gilt on the Cornish gingerbread.

There were photographs on the walls: D.H. Lawrence with Frieda, Middleton Murry with Katherine Mansfield, Maynard Keynes, Lytton Strachey, Duncan Grant, the Woolfs – all taken on the balcony outside the very room where he now sat. Virginia Woolf's genuine original lighthouse, setting aside all Hebridean substitutes, was just a few miles up the coast. And cheek-by-jowl with the photographs were paintings given to his father or to him by notables of the St Ives and Newlyn schools. There was a single portrait, the head and shoulders of a young woman with auburn hair coiled on the top of her head like a coronet. The frame carried a little plaque: Ursula 1929.

A knock at the door. Joseph roused himself, adjusted his glasses and closed the book on his finger. 'Come in!'

His son, Ernest.

The old man said, 'You're home early!'

'Charlie Wycliffe is arriving this afternoon and I thought I'd better be here to welcome him.'

At forty-five Ernest had only to look at his father to see what he would himself become in another thirty years – if he lived that long. The Bishop line must have accumulated a hoard of dominant genes; their men were tall, thin, and long-boned, with a tendency to early baldness. And so far, through several generations, they had shown a marked aptitude for survival in a changing world.

'Do you mind if I help myself to a sherry?' Ernest went to a little cupboard and lifted out a tray with a bottle of Tio Pepe and glasses. 'Will you join me, father?'

'I've just had my lunch. Have you got something on your mind?'

Ernest poured himself a glass of sherry. 'I had a visitor in the office this morning. Who do you think?'

16

His father made an irritable movement. 'I've never been any good at guessing games, Ernest. Get on with it!'

'Lemarque.'

He had the satisfaction of seeing the old man surprised. 'Lemarque? What did he want?'

'He came about the cottage.'

'They're moving out.'

'On the contrary. He gave me a cheque to cover the rent for the two years during which, as he put it, "I was detained elsewhere". Of course I said there was no need but he insisted.'

'And?'

'He said he wanted to continue the tenancy for at least a year and he suggested an agreement. He said he would understand if we wanted to raise the rent and that he would pay what was reasonable.'

Joseph stroked his silky moustache. 'Extraordinary! What's behind it? Why didn't he come here?'

'I suppose he wasn't too sure of his welcome and he wanted to keep it business-like.'

'I haven't seen him since he came out, how does he look?'

'I don't think he's suffered unduly from the slings and arrows but he's drinking; he's got that look. Apart from anything else it was just before one when he came to see me and he was smelling of whisky then.'

The old man shook his head. 'I don't understand what he's up to. What did you say to him?'

'That they are more than welcome to stay on in the cottage for as long as it suits them but that we would prefer not to enter into any formal agreement.'

'All you could say. This scheme he's supposed to be involved with, do you know anything about it?'

'Only that it's in some way connected with Rosemergy Minerals.'

'That's Tim Trewhella; you should talk to Tim.'

'I have, and I'm no wiser.'

Joseph sighed. 'Curiouser and curiouser! Have you mentioned this to Caroline?'

'Not yet.'

'Then don't. Have a quiet word with Gerald when he comes; we don't want any upset over Christmas.'

Ernest drained his glass. 'I'm wondering if this is in some way to do with Gerald.'

'Why should it be?'

'At the time, Lemarque said he had enough evidence to take Gerald to jail with him.'

A dry laugh. 'Just talk! You've always had a tendency to believe what people say, Ernest. Fatal in our profession. But even if Lemarque was speaking the truth he's missed the boat. He's left it too late.'

'Too late to put Gerry in jail, perhaps, but not too late to throw a spanner in his political works, or at least to threaten to.'

'Blackmail?' The old man dismissed the idea. 'You're dramatizing the situation! All the same I'd be interested to know what Rosemergy Minerals can do for Lemarque and even more in what they think he can do for them.'

Ernest said: 'I don't like the idea of him settling here. Whatever we say in the interests of the family, you and I know that Lemarque is a very clever rogue though not quite clever enough. Gerald was mixed up in his shady business and he was lucky to get out of it without a major scandal. All I'm saying is that I hope we're not going to get the scandal now.'

Joseph brushed the notion aside. 'You worry too much, Ernest! Relax!'

Ernest stood up, still holding his empty glass. 'I'll take this down. Don't forget we've got Wycliffe with us for dinner this evening.'

'I'm not yet totally senile, Ernest. As a matter of fact, I'm looking forward to meeting the man. What's he like? Will he get on with Carrie and Vee?'

'If he doesn't, it won't be his fault.'

A broad grin. 'You'll have to keep Gerald out of his hair.'

'I think Charles can take care of himself.'

Joseph, now thoroughly roused from his lethargy, said: 'Good! I feel I'm going to have a nice Christmas. Tell Ada I intend to be hungry tonight.'

CHAPTER TWO

'Turn left here unless you're going through St Ives.' Wycliffe muttered the words. It was what Helen would have said had she been with him. But Helen was far away in Kenya, staying with their newly married son who had a job there. In a year or two they would be grandparents. Salutary thought! As a couple they were post-reproductive, being gently but surely edged aside by the mainstream of existence. Perhaps the slippered pantaloon bit was still some way off but one saw it coming. He found wry consolation in the thought that he must be in Shakespeare's fifth stage: 'the justice, In fair round belly with good capon lined . . . full of wise saws and modern instances.' Not so wide of the mark for he was on his way to spend Christmas with Ernest Bishop, a lawyer with a practice in Penzance.

Wycliffe did not even know him very well; they had met in the courts and on various committees. During a three-day conference Bishop had stayed with the Wycliffes, now he was repaying the hospitality debt. Quiet, reserved, with a wicked wit, his comments on the law and its practitioners were trenchant and amusing. He had a curious hobby which was characteristic of him: he collected and studied flies.

But Wycliffe was not at all keen on the prospect. Ernest was a bachelor and the house was run by his two sisters, one of whom was married to Gerald Bateman, M.P., so that the position of Ernest's guest might be uncomfortably peripheral.

Three o'clock and raining out of a sombre sky; hardly any traffic, but when another car did pass, the bow waves sprayed both vehicles. Dipped headlights and the screen-wipers rocking. He climbed the slope outflanking Trencrom Hill and came out at last on the coast road. Another three or four miles.

The sea on his right, the granite moorland on his left, a bleak landscape where the men of Bronze built strange megaliths for their dead and the men of Iron had seemed content to live in their thatched huts and cultivate their little fields. The dimly shining strip of road rose and fell like a miniature switchback, complicated by meanders orginally plotted by medieval cattle. An early nineteenth-century traveller got it about right: 'the moorstone or granite lies dispersed in detached blocks, many of them huge enough for another Stonehenge. Scarcely a shrub appears to diversify the prospect; and the only living beings that inhabit the mountainous parts are goats . . .' Wycliffe saw no goats.

Suddenly he was there; houses on both sides of the road – the village of Mulfra, a mining village when there were mines. The houses, mostly small, were strung out along the coast road and clustered round the church; black soil, granite walls, and slate roofs covered with grey lichen. The church tower, four-square, no non-sense, and forty feet high, to remind hardened hearts of the all-seeing eye. Some of the villagers had tried to ameliorate this stark severity with gaily painted front doors and bits of scrolled ironwork but they would have had more success with paper chains in a morgue.

Ernest's letter had said that he must turn down by the pub. He spotted a narrow gap between pub and cottage and a blue and white wall sign which read: 'To Mulfra Headland and Cove.' The pub was The Tributers and Wycliffe prided himself (a foreigner) on knowing that tributers were 'free' miners working under contract for the adventurers. Cornishmen avoided being wage slaves whenever they could.

A few more cottages and the road degenerated to a dirt track between low granite walls. Another cottage, standing alone, and the track became even rougher with a rising boulder-strewn slope on one side and a shallow reedy valley on the other. A sudden twist in the track and he had arrived. Mynhager House was perched on a ledge above the sea, stark against a darkening sky, but there were lights in several of the windows.

He pulled into a paved courtyard, muttering to himself: 'I'm not looking forward to this.'

A door from the house opened and Ernest Bishop in a shabby waterproof and a cap came across to him. 'Charles! So very pleasant to see you again! No use apologizing for the weather, it's what we expect here at this time of the year.'

Ernest insisted on carrying his suitcase and led him through a short passage into the front hall. He dropped the suitcase and pulled a grubby white handkerchief from the pocket of his raincoat to wipe his glasses. With the handkerchief came a little shower of glass specimen tubes. Ernest picked them up, smiling. 'For my flies. I'm never without them.'

Wycliffe was introduced to a dark haired woman in her late thirties. 'My sister, Mrs Bateman.' Ernest smiled. 'Caroline to you, I think.'

Caroline was running to fat and she had that pouting, slightly sullen expression of the spoiled self-indulgent woman. Her greeting was polite but without warmth. 'I expect you would like to go to your room and freshen up . . . I hope you will be comfortable.'

He was given a front bedroom overlooking the sea and the cove. A huge Victorian wardrobe, a dressing table, a chest of drawers, a monumental brass bedstead and a couple of armchairs, still left plenty of room on the well-worn Wilton.

Caroline said, 'There's only a shared bathroom, through that door.' She laughed. 'As long as you secure yourself from the other side you'll be all right. If there's anything you want don't hesitate to say.'

At the door she turned back. 'Oh, do come down to

22

the dining-room when you're ready. Make yourself at home. This evening we shall have our meal early because some of the family go to the Song Play at the church, a thing the vicar does every Christmas. I know it sounds awful but they do it quite well and you might even enjoy it.'

So far so good!

He put his hand on a massive old-fashioned radiator which looked as though it had been built for the Albert Hall. It was hot. There was a washbasin and two rough turkish towels on a heated towel rail. Things could have been a lot worse. He walked over to the window; almost dark. He could see a paved terrace below the window, then a steep slope of forty or fifty feet to the sea. It was calm and the gentle surge of the dark water could be detected only in the changing pattern of reflections from its surface. To his left he could just make out the cove which seemed to be choked with leg-trapping boulders.

Half-an-hour later he went downstairs, hair combed, hands clean, and washed behind the ears. Ernest was hovering in the hall, a nervous host.

'There you are, Charles! Come into the drawing-room, you must be longing for a cup of tea.'

In the large, time-worn drawing-room Caroline was standing by the fire talking to her husband who was seated in one of the armchairs and Wycliffe had the impression that their conversation had not been amicable. Gerald Bateman M.P., known to everyone for his TV appearances, always ready with concise, dogmatic pronouncements on any issue from genetic engineering to the decline of flax growing on St Helena: 'My dear Robin (or Brian, or John), I fully appreciate the complexity of the problem but . . .' His real hobby horse was Law and Order: the Supremacy of the Law, Individual Responsibility, Justice, and Punishment.

In the corridors of power they called him The Sheriff, but behind the political façade there was a thin-lipped

23

intelligence which had enabled him to keep head and shoulders well above water through the recession.

Ernest said: 'You've already met Caroline; this is her husband. No introduction necessary, I'm sure.'

Bateman sprang to his feet with instant charm: 'My dear Mr Wycliffe! This is a real pleasure. I'm quite sure we shall have some interesting talks while you are here; interesting and instructive for me at any rate.'

Ernest said: 'Gerald is anxious to brief himself for a debate on the crime statistics when the House reassembles. Remember, Charles, you do not have to say anything but whatever you do say may be taken down and used in his speech.'

Bateman smiled. 'Ernest must have his little joke; it is a family idiosyncrasy.'

Bateman was forty-six, tall, with a youthful figure, and good looking in the clean-limbed, manly virtues fashion: dark hair well cut, carefully trimmed guards' moustache, and perfectly shaved.

Ernest turned to his sister: 'See if you can hurry up Virginia with the tea, dear.'

A tall, elderly woman made an entrance. No question that she was a Bishop: big boned, spare, with angular features and deep-set eyes. She wore a mauve satin frock, badly creased, an orange silk scarf loosely knotted, and her grey hair had a wispy wildness. The White Queen straight out of Alice.

Ernest hastened to introduce her. 'Mrs Burnett-Price, my Aunt Stella: Chief Superintendent Wycliffe.'

The old lady acknowledged the introduction with gravity then went on: 'I'm so glad you are here though it surprises me that they should send a chief superintendent to deal with a few instances of pilfering. However, as my husband used to say: "The army has its own way of doing things" and I suppose it is the same with the police.' She laughed, still a musical sound; she must have been a charmer in her day.

An imploring look from Ernest. Wycliffe merely

nodded and looked amiable. Ernest conducted his aunt to a straight backed chair near the fire.

Tea arrived on a trolley, with Virginia, a younger, slimmer version of her sister.

'Two more members of the family still to meet,' Ernest said. 'Father, who doesn't put in an appearance until we sit down to our evening meal, and my nephew Paul, of whom the same can usually be said.'

Tea and little rock cakes which had spent too long in the oven. Ernest said: 'I don't know if Caroline mentioned the vicar's play which is on this evening . . . I usually go, so do Virginia and Paul. I wondered if you might be interested?'

Wycliffe protested that he was looking forward to it.

In what promised to be a stilted conversation with Caroline he happened to mention the piano, by far the most elegant piece of furniture in the room, and she warmed to him at once.

'It's a Steinway, and it's mine; father indulged me terribly when I showed some talent for music. It wasn't literature, which would have pleased him more, but it was something to have a daughter who would make a name for herself in music. Of course, I never did. All the same, it's my one claim to any sort of culture.' She laughed. 'Pictures, sculpture, literature, and even gourmet eating, leave me cold, but music . . . Music to me is like sex; with the advantage that it lasts longer and they tell me you can still enjoy it in old age.'

Wycliffe realized that he had been received into that circle of acquaintances with whom Caroline found it amusing to flirt.

Bateman, left out, stood alone looking patient, like a well-mannered Doberman waiting to be noticed and patted. Obviously the distinguished politician cut little ice at Mynhager.

When Caroline was called to the kitchen she was replaced by Virginia; the Bishops were not neglecting their guest. He was briefed on the family and the house.

25

'The house was built by my great-great-grandfather. The Bishops have always been slightly crazy. They made money out of tin and banking, and building Mynhager was their bizarre way of proving that they had it. Then my grandfather imported culture; he was a Cambridge Apostle and this place became a sort of Cornish outpost for the Bloomsbury Set.'

Virginia talked with animation and from time to time she glanced up at him with a disarming grin as though apologizing for her chatter. 'I even owe my name to Virginia Woolf of blessed memory who delighted grandfather by sending him pre-publication copies of her novels.'

Unexpectedly Aunt Stella weighed in from her chair by the fire: 'My husband used to call them "a pack of left-wing intellectuals, ready to bite the hands that fed them." He couldn't bear to stay in the house when any of them were here. And that included poor Arnold Forster who was such a nice man and, although he was a socialist, really quite civilized. He wrote a book about gardening in this part of the world and he lived at Eagle's Nest, just up the coast from here.'

Virginia said, as though in total explanation: 'Uncle George was in the army.'

'Your uncle was a major general, my dear,' Aunt Stella amended.

They had their meal at six and Wycliffe met Joseph, head of the family, and young Paul, for the first time. The old man was an earlier edition of Ernest: tall, spare, amiable, and with a caustic wit. By the same token the seventeen-year-old Paul was every inch another Bishop. Wycliffe wondered how Bateman came to terms with the fact that his paternal contribution had been so effectively swamped.

During the meal Joseph, in a relaxed mood, told stories of village feuds in the Cornwall of sixty years ago and wound up: 'I tell you, Wycliffe, they were a sombre lot around here and they still are. Wesley spread a veneer of religion over 'em but he didn't change the nature of the beast.'

Afterwards, Ernest said, 'Virginia and Paul are going to pick up Jane Lemarque and her daughter, Francine. The Lemarques live in a little house on the other side of the valley, and Francine is playing the Virgin in tonight's play.'

So Wycliffe went with Ernest in his ancient, 3-litre Rover which the family called 'The Hearse'. Ernest drove through the darkness and the mist with the caution appropriate to an acrobat balancing a pretty girl in a wheelbarrow on the high wire.

'I must apologize, Charles, for not warning you about Aunt Stella. Since George died she's been a bit queer in the head. She hides things, forgets where she's put them, then imagines they've been stolen. But it isn't all genuine. She's not above putting on an act for the fun of it, as she did this evening.' Ernest laughed: 'You may have gathered that some of the family have a peculiar sense of humour.'

They reached the church well before eight when the play was due to begin; the bells were ringing a peal. The leafless sycamores in the churchyard made weird shapes and shadows and there was a misty halo around the lamp over the church porch. People were arriving in a thin but steady stream. Virginia and Paul were already in their seats with another woman, an attractive brunette. As they filed into the same pew, Ernest murmured introductions: 'Mrs Jane Lemarque, Mr Wycliffe . . . Francine, Jane's daughter, is the star this evening.'

The dark woman smiled, the closed smile of a nun.

Wycliffe found himself between Ernest and his sister. A large man with a mass of curly black hair came in and sat a couple of seats in front of them.

Ernest said: 'That chap who's just come in – the big fellow who looks like a gipsy, that's Marsden, our local

27

painter – I wonder why he's here; I wouldn't have said this was his sort of thing, would you, Vee?'

'I've no idea!'

Wycliffe thought she had snubbed her brother and wondered why.

The bells stopped ringing, the hushed conversations died away, the organ played a melancholy little tune of single notes, like a pipe; the lights dimmed and went out. For a long moment the church was in total darkness then a light in the form of a star came on over the chancel. A large suspended backdrop hid the altar and was illuminated from behind by slowly changing coloured lights: green to blue, to mauve to violet . . . There was no one to be seen, but a girl's voice sang, sweet and true and unaccompanied:

'I cannot rest beloved, fear steals away my sleep;
    Why should a humble maiden have such a trust
      to keep?
    Did I but dream of the Angel, did I but think
      him there?
    How can I hope that my body the infant Christ
      will bear?'

A baritone voice answered:

'Be not afraid, sweet Mary; queen among women,
      blest;
    God and His Holy Angels shall set your fears at
      rest.
    High in the heaven above us the natal star doth
      shine,
    Token that God in His mercy will grant the gift
      divine.'

Came the inevitable duet. A trite little song, simply and honestly sung, but in the old parish church with no performers in view, and no set, only the empty chancel and the discreetly changing hues of the backdrop, the audience was caught and held.

Darkness once more, then the star.

Mary, seen now, in a simple blue dress with her baby on her lap. She had red-gold hair, like the Renaissance madonnas, coiled loosely on the top of her head. As she bent over the child it caught the light and there was the suggestion of a halo. She sang a plaintive cradle song and an invisible choir brought the glad news to the shepherds. 'Glory to God in the highest and on earth peace, good will toward men.'

The shepherds, first seen as shadows on the backdrop growing in size, came into view singing lustily like Disney's dwarfs. The clowns of the piece, three folklore rustics, they became silent and subdued in the presence of the girl with her baby. Shyly, they handed her their tributes – three posies of wild flowers, and gravely she took them, one at a time, and said: 'White flowers for Innocence . . . red for Majesty . . . ' And after a long pause, and in a low voice, 'and purple for Death.'

In that moment Wycliffe felt that he had glimpsed the forgotten magic of Christmas.

Solemn organ music heralded the approach of the kings as their shadows grew larger. They introduced themselves with courtly manners and in elegant language spoke of the star they had seen in the east. They foretold the greatness of the child and presented their gifts.

Mary received them, saying: 'From Melchior, Gold for Royalty . . . From Caspar, Frankincense for Divinity . . . ' And in a low voice which seemed to falter: 'From Balthazar, Myrrh for Death.'

She thanked them and the kings departed. Joseph had his dream in which he was warned by an angel of Herod's intent and the play ended with the Holy Family setting out on the flight into Egypt. Mary sang her final song which was a prayer for their safety.

Wycliffe was moved and deeply impressed, in particular by the girl. She had seemed quite unaware of her audience. With scarcely any movement and with an expression of grave wonder, she had allowed the action to take place about her but leaving no one in any doubt that she was the still centre and focus of it all.

It had lasted an hour and when the vicar gave his benediction the audience sat on for a while as though reluctant to come back into the real world. Wycliffe turned to congratulate Jane on her daughter's performance but she had already left the pew.

Paul said: 'Mrs Lemarque has gone to the vestry to help Francine. If you will excuse me . . . '

Ernest laughed. 'Poor lad! After tonight he'll be in deeper than ever. Anyway, there are refreshments in the church room; if we go along we shall be able to meet the vicar and his cast. What about it?'

'I'd like to meet that girl,' Wycliffe said.

Ernest was pleased. 'Better than all the tinsel and shiny balls, don't you think? A little magic now and then for thy soul's sake.' He sighed. 'Francine is a very talented girl, but difficult.'

Outside the rain had stopped, it was very dark and still and the air was fresh with the tang of salt.

The church hall was a converted barn, clean but spartan; dedicated women stood behind trestle tables selling tea, coffee, and sausage rolls in aid of the church restoration fund. Within a remarkably short space of time seventy or eightly people were clustered in groups, each with a cup and saucer in one hand and a sausage roll in the other. The vicar, at the centre of the largest group, towered head and shoulders above them, lean, blond and saintly.

'He's not liked by everyone,' Virginia said. 'For one thing he's a bachelor and that doesn't suit, then he's too "high" for some: confession, incense, and all that sort of thing, but he's a clever man, and a kind one.'

30

'Ah, Miss Bishop!' The vicar ploughed through to speak to Virginia. 'Mrs Lemarque asked me to pass on her apology. Francine is being difficult again. It seems that as soon as our play ended she changed back into her ordinary clothes and walked out.'

'Walked out? But where has she gone?'

'Home, presumably. Her mother is very upset and insisted on going home herself. I begged her to wait, then Paul wanted to drive her home but she wouldn't hear of it.' The vicar smiled. 'I think there will be some straight talking in the Lemarque household tonight. A pity!'

'But what was the matter with Francine?'

The vicar raised his hands. 'What is ever the matter with Francine? I suppose we must allow for temperament but really I think she should have stayed. Everyone wants to congratulate her, we have two reporters here, and I know that the Women's Guild have a very nice present for her.'

Somebody said: 'Was she holding a real baby? Once I thought I heard it whimper.'

The vicar smiled. 'No, not a real baby; that was Francine's black doll. It seems to be her mascot.'

'A black doll?'

'Why not? Apart from any other consideration they tell us that our Lord probably had a dusky skin.'

Wycliffe was introduced to the vicar and he met the rest of the cast, all a little flustered by success: Joseph, a local farmer's son; the shepherds, members of an amateur pop group; the three kings, the choir . . .

As the church clock was striking ten Wycliffe and Ernest were walking back to the car and in The Tributers they were singing "Good King Wenceslas" with variations.

The drawing-room at Mynhager looked as festive as it was ever likely to. A good fire burned in the large open

31

grate which Ernest called 'The Miners' Friend', though tonight it was burning logs.

Joseph had stayed up later than usual in deference to their guest and everyone was drinking. Joseph nursed a glass of port which he frequently replenished. Wycliffe, Gerald Bateman and Caroline drank whisky; Virginia, Paul and the elusive Ada drank white wine. Ernest had lime juice. It was the first time Wycliffe had seen Ada: a plump, energetic little woman of sixty-five with remarkably clear skin, and grey hair gathered into a bun on the top of her head.

Between sips of gin and tonic, Aunt Stella knitted. A long, scarf-like strip depended from her needles, overflowed her lap and reached for the floor. Wycliffe was reminded of Madame Defarge at the foot of the guillotine.

Caroline, watched by her husband, sprawled in one of the armchairs, showing a great deal of thigh; she had put away several whiskies and Wycliffe judged that she was drunk enough to cause a scene if Bateman attempted to interfere.

They talked about the 'festive season' and the inability of the English to celebrate; the Anglo Saxon's failure to overcome his inhibitions and let his hair down.

'Except in outbursts of drunken violence' – Virginia.

'Imagine Mardi Gras in Malvern' – Ernest.

Aunt Stella began: 'When George and I were in Madras . . .' But the memory, whatever it was, faded, and she lapsed into silence.

Paul said: 'At least we have Notting Hill.'

His father was derisive. 'The West Indians are responsible for that, it's their show. As far as Europeans are concerned it's only in those countries with a Catholic tradition that you get the true spirit of carnival.'

'Nonsense!' Joseph obviously welcomed a chance to challenge his son-in-law. 'Catholic, Protestant, Jew or atheist, it makes no difference: celebration and self-denial or deprivation are two sides of the same coin. Ash Wednesday follows Shrove Tuesday; Easter Day follows Good Friday; there's no satisfaction – no joy, in the one without the other. Of course we can deceive ourselves. As a nation we've become pathologically self-indulgent but we pay the price in a joyless existence of boredom and frustration.'

The old man's eyes sparkled from the port he had drunk. 'Look at us now, preparing to celebrate the birth of our Lord; each one of us with a quiet determination to take aboard enough alcohol to enable us to endure the boredom until bedtime!' He turned to Wycliffe, 'Isn't that so?'

Wycliffe smiled. 'I'm certainly not bored.'

The old man laughed. 'No, I can believe that. For an observer of human nature a family like ours is better than a whole load of case-books.'

In an uncomfortable silence Paul said: 'I think I'll go to bed. Good night everybody.'

A chorus of good nights. A welcome signal for the party to break up.

Wycliffe climbed into the great bed and snuggled down under the blankets. A strange family! But aren't all families a bit odd seen from the inside?

He thought of Helen, living it up somewhere in the Kenyan highlands and wondered what the weather was like. Anyway she would be in bed; it would be three o'clock in the morning. Silently he wished her good night.

He lay there listening to the tide surging and chuckling between the boulders in the cove, then sucking back. As he listened the sounds seemed to get louder. He tried to imagine what it would be like in a Force 10 nor' westerly when those boulders must grind together like the mills of God.

'White flowers for Innocence . . .' The words came back to him and with them a vivid mind-picture of the

33

girl. There was something about her . . . How old was she? Seventeen? Eighteen, perhaps? – not more . . . Lemarque; they must be of French extraction . . . No mention of a father . . . He hoped there would be a chance to meet her . . .

'. . . and purple for Death.' How absurd! He could not get the girl or the play out of his mind.

He fell asleep still thinking of Francine.

CHAPTER THREE

Christmas Eve Morning. Wycliffe went out on to the terrace and stood, arms resting on the balustrade. Further along a herring-gull perched on one leg, motionless. The weather was sunny and still. He was missing his after-breakfast pipe; a fortnight of abstinence had convinced him that this was the time of day when resistance was at its lowest ebb. Virginia came out of the house and the gull launched itself into the air with an angry squawk.

'Good morning! Lovely day!'

She wore a fluffy woollen jumper and a matching skirt. Wycliffe thought she looked young, fresh, and wholesome; sorting through his stock of adjectives he might have conceded pretty. She joined him, arms resting on the balustrade.

'Wonderfully mild for the time of year, isn't it?'

She was dark, with freckles which stopped short of her eyes and reminded him that this was the first time he had seen her without her glasses. They stood, looking down into the water, so clear they could see the yellow sandy bottom with a school of small fish darting and wheeling above it like a flock of starlings in the air.

'Is the sand uncovered at low tide?'

'No, thank goodness! If it was we should be overrun with trippers in the season.'

A fishing boat rounded Gurnard's Head and cruised parallel with the shore.

'Half-decked St Ives gig,' Virginia said, showing off. 'That'll be the *Jennifer*, Bert Gundry's boat; he takes us out now and then.'

A figure at the tiller raised a hand in salute and she waved back.

'Fishing, another dying industry in these parts.' She pointed across to the ruins of a mine stack and engine house jutting up like a broken tooth from one of the smaller promontories. 'Tin, copper and fish, the three-legged Cornish stool. The first two have dropped off and the third is suffering from Common Market disease; so we sit back and watch our county being destroyed by tourism.'

Wycliffe chuckled. 'A sombre diagnosis.'

'A plain statement of fact.'

'Isn't that Ernest over there?' Wycliffe pointed across the inlet to a rocky beach strewn with kelp washed up by the tide. A crouching man in a khaki waterproof seemed totally absorbed in turning over the weed.

'He's looking for flies.'

'At this time of year?'

Virginia laughed. 'I don't know much about the group but I think quite a few species are about in winter, especially in a mild spell like this. In any case there are larvae which live between the tide lines.'

Wycliffe said: 'Interesting, don't you think? The things people choose to do as opposed to the things they have to do to get a living.'

'Yes. But the lucky ones make a livelihood out of their interest. Ernest became a lawyer because it was expected of him, but he's a good naturalist and might have made a good biologist. Did you choose to be a policeman?'

'I'm afraid I did.'

'Why? Not because you enjoy ordering people about; you obviously don't.'

Even his wife had never asked him such a direct question and he was embarrassed, but he had raised the subject. 'When I was young I didn't quite know why, but as I've got older I've realized that I have a horror of disorder; the prospect of anarchy appals me and I suppose I feel I'm helping to stave it off.'

She looked at him in surprise. 'You see anarchy as an immediate threat?'

'Sometimes I feel that we live in a house of cards and the thought gives me nightmares.'

At that moment Paul came out of the house and, with a brief apology to Wycliffe, approached his aunt. He looked worried.

'I tried to ring Francine, but she isn't there and her mother says it seems she didn't come home last night.'

Virginia was incisive. 'Seems? Doesn't she know?'

'Apparently Mr Lemarque was in bed when Mrs Lemarque got home from the church and she thought Francine must have gone to bed too. It wasn't until half-an-hour ago, when they called Francine and she didn't answer, that they realized she wasn't in her room. Her bed hadn't been slept in.'

'Haven't they any idea where she might be?'

'Mrs Lemarque thinks she's gone to stay with a school friend; she says she's done it before.'

'Without a word to her parents?'

'I think so, yes.'

'Are they making enquiries among her friends?'

Helplessness and frustration got the better of the boy. 'I don't know what they're doing. Nothing, I expect!'

Virginia took pity on her nephew. 'Would you like me to look in and try to be helpful?'

'Would you, Vee?' Aunt and nephew were clearly on good terms.

'Tell your mother that Mr Wycliffe and I are going for a walk but I shall be back in plenty of time to help with the lunch.'

'I don't suppose I can do anything?'

She grinned up at him. 'No, you just stay here and worry.'

She watched the boy return to the house. 'Poor lad! He's in a bad way.'

Wycliffe said: 'You can't want me with you.'

'Why not? I'd like you to meet the Lemarques. I'll get a coat and you could probably do with one.'

As they walked along the track away from Mynhager she pointed out the Lemarques' cottage on the other side of the valley.

'It belongs to us and originally we let it to Alain only as a weekend place. At that time he and Gerald were partners in a London company with a chain of antique shops and picture galleries, doing very well; then things went badly wrong. Alain was a good businessman but it seems he didn't know when he was beaten. Gerald got out, but Lemarque dug himself in deeper and deeper until he finished up in jail for fraud. He came out a few weeks ago.'

'Are they French?'

'Alain's father came over with de Gaulle and stayed. Jane is English and Francine was born in Richmond where they lived when they had money. They lost everything and now the cottage is the only home they have.'

'Hard on the wife and child.'

'It is, very.'

'How old is Francine?'

'Just sixteen; she had a birthday last month.'

'Sixteen! Surely her parents should be taking this more seriously?'

'Yes, you would think so but Jane may be right. Francine is a talented girl but difficult. Like a lot of young people these days she's got a keen sense of justice and if she thought she had a real grievance I wouldn't put it past her to walk out like this.' She laughed. 'Young Paul will have his problems if their friendship ever comes to anything but I don't think it will. Francine gives him very little encouragement.'

Wycliffe was intrigued by Virginia's uninhibited but amiable gossip. There is an appealing innocence about the virgin schoolgirl turned virgin teacher.

38

They were approaching another cottage, standing alone, just a yard or two back from the dirt road. Music came from inside: old-style jazz played very loud.

'That's Marsden's place, the painter; you saw him in church last night.'

'Does he live alone?'

'With a succession of different women; the present one's been there several months, longer than most; usually they come and go in a matter of weeks. He's our scapegoat for scandal; very convenient, I suppose, but we could well do without him. There's been talk recently of Francine going to the cottage when the woman is away at work.' Virginia made a little gesture of distaste. 'I doubt if there's any more substance in that than there is in most of the gossip round here. You know what villages are. All the same it's very unpleasant.'

The sunshine heightened colours in the landscape, the drab green of heather and gorse, the red-brown splashes of dead bracken, and the grey-white boulders. But out to sea black clouds were creeping up the sky.

'Of course, a lot of Francine's trouble is that she reacts against her mother.'

'Why against her mother?'

Virginia considered. 'Jane is a difficult woman to live with; she seems to carry about her an aura of sadness, as though she were in perpetual mourning for somebody or something.'

'Is this because of her husband going to jail?'

'No. She's been like that for years. Odd, really, she used to be such a cheerful girl when we first knew her. She's never been the same since Francine was born.'

They turned off down the steep slope which led to the footbridge and because it was narrow they had to walk in single file.

On the other side she went on: 'It's hard to explain. Jane is the most passive of women, if passive is the right word, but if I had to live with her I'd probably end up by doing something dramatic and stupid like Francine, just to provoke a response.'

So Francine was barely sixteen, he had thought her older.

The Lemarques' cottage, weathered and grey, seemed to have grown out of the hillside, a larger version of the granite boulders which littered the slope. Parked at the bottom of the steps which led up to the front door was a small grey van, several years old, with patches of red paint on the grey to cope with rust.

'Poor Alain used to drive a Jaguar,' Virginia said. 'A new one every couple of years.'

Jane Lemarque must have seen them from the window for as they reached the other side of the footbridge the front door opened and she was standing at the top of the steps. Dark hair and blue eyes, a pale oval face with high cheek bones. Beauty without artifice, perhaps without awareness.

'Compliments of the season, Jane!' Virginia could hardly wish her a merry Christmas. 'Paul told us about Francine and as we were out for a walk I thought we might look in and see if we could be of any help.'

'You're a stranger, Vee! Do come in.'

The words were welcoming but the voice was flat and indifferent; the beautiful face was not exactly vacant but unresponsive.

They were shown into the living-room, characterless and uncared for. A coal fire burned half-heartedly in the grate. No Christmas decorations, no tree; the only sign of Christmas, a number of cards arranged on the mantelpiece. In the adjoining kitchen something simmering on the stove gave off little jets of steam and an unappetizing smell.

'I'll call Alain.' She called him, standing at the bottom of the stairs. 'Virginia is here, Alain. With a friend.'

Alain came down the stairs; a small man, very dark, swarthy. At first sight Wycliffe thought that he must have seen the man before, then he realized that he was recognizing a type, a genus. Lemarque had the sad, deeply furrowed yet mobile face of a clown. His manner was uneasy, a man not at home in his own house.

'Hullo, Vee!' Sheepish.

Wycliffe was introduced. At close quarters he noticed a slight reddening around the mouth and nose. A whisky flush? If so it had been acquired in a few weeks.

'You haven't come about my daughter?' Suspicious.

It struck Wycliffe as odd that this strange little man could claim Francine as his daughter. He said: 'No, I happened to be staying at Mynhager and we were out for a walk.'

Virginia, insensitive to the pitfalls of social contact between an ex-con and an officer of the C.I.D., ploughed in: 'But Mr Wycliffe could be very helpful if you decided to call in the police.'

Lemarque looked at his wife. 'Jane says she's done this before, while I've been away.'

Jane said nothing now. She sat bolt upright and quite still, her gaze fixed on the fireplace. Her hands were clasped so tightly together in her lap that her arms seemed to tremble. Safety valve screwed right down.

But she was beautiful. Watching her, Wycliffe had unchaste thoughts, though it might be like sleeping with a sphinx. Probably only Lemarque had had the chance to find out. But agile little men, simian types, are often proud of their sexual prowess. Would Lemarque have been content with a frigid wife? Anyhow the hazards of sexual selection and the genetic lottery had produced Francine. Irrelevant thoughts of a chief superintendent.

Virginia was saying: 'Why does she do it – go off without a word?'

Jane said: 'To punish me.' The words seemed to escape almost against her will.

'To punish you, Jane? Surely not!' Virginia.

Lemarque glanced quickly at Wycliffe and away again.

Silence.

Virginia tried to bridge the gap with words. 'I'm sure Francine is quite safe but, if you don't hear today, think how worried you'll be; and all that time lost!'

Wycliffe felt that the tension had little to do with the missing girl. They were like actors playing a part while preoccupied with their real lives. There was no rapport between man and wife or between them and their drab surroundings. More than once Wycliffe saw the woman's lips moving as though in prayer.

The room was a collection of odds and ends; nothing chosen or valued or cared for. The little window looked out across the valley and from where Wycliffe sat there was no sky to be seen, only the dun-coloured and barren hillside opposite. A dismal, lonely prospect. What did the woman do all day when her husband was away? No books, magazines or newspapers; no sewing or knitting; not even a television set or a radio.

The silence seemed to challenge someone to break it; even Virginia was subdued. Lemarque said: 'What do you think, Jane?'

'It's up to you.'

They seemed to exist in a limbo of inaction and yet under almost insupportable tension. Lemarque turned to Wycliffe. 'What do we have to do?'

'Nothing at the moment. I'll arrange for someone to come and talk to you about Francine, and the routine enquiries will go ahead.'

With any other parents he would have felt the need to reassure them: 'The police are quite good at this sort of thing; it happens more often than you think so don't worry too much . . .'

He could have telephoned from the cottage; the telephone was there in the living-room but he preferred to wait until he was back at Mynhager. One reason was that he did not want to appear too directly involved.

Jane seemed greatly relieved to see them go; she even came out on to the steps and wished them a happy Christmas.

It was a relief to be once more out in the sunshine. As they were crossing the bridge Wycliffe said: 'An extraordinary couple! It's hard to imagine what life must be like in that . . . that vacuum. And the girl . . . Is Jane Lemarque frightened of something?'

Virginia said: 'She certainly seems worse than she was. I'm really glad you came, they wouldn't have done anything otherwise. What do you think about Francine?'

'What can one think? I very much doubt if she's staying with a school friend. Can you imagine any parent collecting a young girl, late in the evening, without previous contact with her parents?'

'You think something has happened to her?'

'That's what we've got to find out, but her parents know more than they've told us. Do you teach Francine?'

'No, she goes to a different school.'

Unconsciously he was adopting his professional role. He was disturbed.

Back at Mynhager he telephoned Chief Inspector Clarke of Divisional C.I.D. When the conversation was over Clarke put down the telephone, crushed out his half-smoked cigarette and cursed. 'Right on his bloody doorstep, and over Christmas. That's all we needed!'

He picked up the telephone again and called Detective Inspector Wills. 'I've just had the chief super on the line, Jim. He's spending Christmas in Mulfra village with Bishop, the lawyer. Some kid, a girl of sixteen, has gone missing right under his nose. Here are the details, such as they are . . . Ready?' He passed on the information he had. 'It's your patch, Jim, so watch your step. You're to send somebody to talk to the parents pronto, and the governor must be kept informed . . . Didn't Curtis work under him on some case? . . . The undertaker, that's it! Then Curtis is the man for this job. Not that it will amount to much. The kid will be back with mamma, wet and weepy by tonight. But if there's any cock-up, for God's sake let me know and put your head on the block, ready. And a very merry Christmas to you and yours!'

So the file which was not yet a file ended up on the desk of Detective Sergeant Curtis.

'That damned girl is going to spoil your Christmas, Wycliffe. Don't let her! She's only trying to make some impression on her mother. Not that I blame her for that. Lemarque spent years trying to do the same thing and look where it landed him!' The old man chuckled. 'Jane is like Everest, an enduring provocation simply by being there.' He turned to his son-in-law, 'Isn't that so, Gerald?'

They were at lunch and Gerald Bateman was trying to retrieve a small pat of butter from the table cloth without being noticed. He snapped: 'I'm quite sure Jane had nothing whatever to do with Lemarque's troubles.'

Caroline said: 'It wouldn't surprise me if she had gone off with some man, and I mean, man.'

Paul was staring at his plate without eating.

Aunt Stella, appetite unimpaired by age, consumed cheese and biscuits with the concentration and delicacy of a chimpanzee grooming for lice. She broke a water biscuit into four and placed a modicum of cheese on each section. 'If she's gone away then at least she is showing more discretion than most of them do these days.'

There was a noticeable silence then Ernest said with quiet emphasis: 'We are talking about Francine, aunt – Jane's daughter.'

Stella looked surprised. 'Francine? But she's only a child! It's hardly—'

'Francine is sixteen, aunt.'

Stella took into her mouth a portion of biscuit and cheese, patted her lips with a napkin and said: 'Isn't that what I was saying? These days they behave at sixteen as we wouldn't have dared to do at twenty-five!'

44

After the meal Wycliffe said to Ernest: 'I hope you don't mind; I've asked my people to keep me informed here.'

'My dear chap! You're doing us a favour.'

Wycliffe felt drowsy; the unaccustomed combination of whisky before and white wine during lunch was having its effect. He went into the drawing-room where there was a fire in the grate and the presents were laid out like votive offerings round the Christmas tree ready for distribution that night. The room was empty. He settled in one of the easy chairs with a magazine and was slightly embarrassed to wake up and find Ada standing over him.

'Sergeant Curtis wants to see you; I've put him in the dining-room.'

It was half-past three and almost dark. In the gloomy panelled dining-room Ada had switched on the dusty chandelier with its crystal drops.

Wycliffe knew Curtis of old and was pleased to renew the acquaintance. Curtis had the build of a heavyweight wrestler, with a great moon-like face in which eyes, nose and mouth were grouped together like palm trees in a desert oasis. A man of few words, he supplemented speech with gesture which sometimes reached the level of mime. He took a notebook from his pocket and placed it on the table but Wycliffe knew that he would not refer to it.

'I talked to madame; monsieur was out.' The huge hands seemed to pluck little manikins from the air and present them for inspection. 'They've no idea where or why the girl might have gone. Extraordinary! The woman seems to know nothing about her own daughter, about her school, her teachers or her friends . . . '

Curtis stared at the ceiling. 'I tried to find out what could have made the girl go off. Something must have. Had there been a row? "We don't have rows" madame informed me.' Curtis looked wide-eyed. 'Funny family in that case! Of course I suppose it's possible the girl was abducted but that hardly seems likely to me.

45

'I asked about friends visiting the house, letters . . . Friends don't visit, madame told me, but Francine does have letters occasionally. Big deal! Who from? Where from? . . . The silly woman doesn't have a clue. "We don't spy on our daughter."' Curtis heaved a profound sigh. 'Neither did we on ours but we made damn sure we had some idea of what she was up to. I looked at the cards on the mantelpiece – most of 'em were for Francine, all signed with pet names. Unisex. Madame could only tell me about one which came from the Bateman boy and you'll know about him, sir.'

'Did you ask about relatives that she might have gone to?'

'It seems that Lemarque has no relatives in this country that he is in contact with.'

'And Jane?'

'She has a sister in Bristol and an aunt in Oxford; they keep in touch more or less, but she says Francine scarcely knows them.'

'Did you see the girl's room?'

'No problem. When I asked, madame said: "Upstairs; the door in front of you". Liberty Hall! Didn't tell me much though.' Curtis sketched a box in the air. 'Poky little room; the usual posters of pop stars on the walls; the usual collection of teenage clobber in the wardrobe and drawers – all looking as though it had been thrown out by Oxfam. When I was young, girls wanted to look pretty. I asked madame if she had taken any clothes with her other than what she wore. Madame (would you believe?) wasn't sure. All she was sure of was that the girl had taken her doll.'

'Her doll?'

'A black-faced doll she's had since she was an infant. She always slept with it in her bed. Our Gwen had a teddy bear which she put on her pillow every night right up to the time she got married. Afterwards too, for all I know.'

'Go on.'

46

Curtis recovered his narrative: 'About her bedroom: there were a few books, all school issue except one on adolescent sex. (I suppose that could be school issue too, these days.) A few tubes of paint, some brushes, and a blank sketch-pad. No pictures of hers or anybody else's. I had the impression she was thumbing her nose at me and at any other snoopers that happened along: "Make something out of this, Buster!"'

Curtis grinned. 'I couldn't and didn't.'

'Did you ask about what money she might have had?'

'I did, sir, but not to much purpose. It seems she had a job as a waitress in St Ives during the last summer holidays but what she earned or what she did with it her mother has no idea. Otherwise mother gave her money as she wanted it for some specific thing.'

'So what is your general impression?'

Curtis closed the notebook to which he had not once referred. 'A planned flit with a deliberate touch of the old melodrama. The day before Christmas Eve, and after playing the star role in the vicar's play, Bingo! the lady vanishes.' A deep sigh. 'Is that how you see it, sir?'

Wycliffe wasn't sure. Curtis's diagnosis seemed reasonable; a gesture of defiance, an expression of frustration, an assertion of independence. Take it out of that.

'You've got a photograph?'

Curtis looked sour. 'Two years out of date.'

'What else have you put in hand?'

'I've got a couple of chaps trying to make contact with her teachers and, through them, with her school friends. The chances are she talked to somebody. A teenage girl who doesn't tell at least some of it to her best friend would be a very rare bird. Of course, she may be just that.' Curtis shook his great head. 'Having Christmas round the corner doesn't make it easier. I found that in the village; characters who would be glad to talk their heads off normally have something better to do.'

'Did you get anything?'

'Not much. Of course you never know what the Cornish think, only what they say, and that's often the family or the village line. In this case they're saying that Francine is no better than she ought to be and that her mother and father are not liked.' Curtis lowered his voice. 'I'm afraid that's true of the Bishops too.'

'Nothing specific on the girl?'

'Just two things. The other members of the cast who were in the vestry when the play ended say she came in, went behind the curtain, changed into her outdoor clothes and left without a word to anybody.'

'And the other thing?'

'A little old woman, living alone . . . ' Curtis's hands somehow conveyed five-feet nothing of skin and bone. 'A real tartar with a tongue like a serpent's tooth. After telling me that a chap called Marsden, a painter, is having it off with half the female population of the district including the girl, she said she saw him talking to Francine last night after the play. They were just beyond the church.'

Marsden: Virginia had mentioned the gossip. Wycliffe said: 'It may not mean much but if he was the last person to be seen with her we'd better talk to him.'

He went into the drawing-room to leave word that he was going out but there was no one there. In the end he found Caroline in the kitchen. She was topping a trifle with little blobs of whipped cream and there was a strong smell of brandy. Ernest was with her, licking his fingers like a guilty schoolboy.

'I'm afraid I have to go out in connection with the Francine business.' He felt like a schoolboy himself, asking permission to leave the room, but Caroline was cheerfully indifferent.

'It's every man for himself until we eat at seven. Don't be late then.'

Wycliffe had to admit to a more than professional interest in this painter who looked like a gipsy, had a

48

reputation as a seducer, and listened to jazz blasted out in megabels.

Curtis was waiting in his car. It was quite dark now with a thin rain which smelled and tasted of the sea. Still no wind. They drove along the track, Curtis hunched over the wheel of his little Fiesta like some giant animal brooding its young. There was light in the painter's window and as soon as the engine cut they could hear the inevitable jazz. Not for the first time, Curtis surprised Wycliffe.

'Benny Goodman's "One o'clock jump"; that takes me back!'

They knocked, then banged on the door until the music was shut off. Heavy footsteps, then the door opened and there was Marsden; monumental against the light, like a Graham Sutherland portrait in 3-D. They introduced themselves.

'You'd better come in.'

The room was spartan. Apart from the record-player in one corner it was little different from how it must have been a century earlier when a Cornish mining family lived there. A floor of blue slate slabs with mats; a large deal table now littered with dirty dishes; and a couple of Windsor armchairs, one on each side of the fire. In one, a tabby cat was asleep, in the other there was an open book, and on the floor by the chair, a bottle of wine and a glass.

Marsden placed two kitchen chairs for his visitors. 'What's this about, then? I suppose I should apologize for the mess but it's the servants' night out. You know how it is with the lower classes these days.'

He spoke in a guttural voice and the words seemed to surface with some difficulty from a great depth.

Wycliffe said: 'I suppose you know that Francine Lemarque is missing?'

Marsden's expression froze. 'Missing? How long since?'

It was Curtis who said: 'Since last night.'

Marsden turned to Curtis. A confrontation between heavyweights; they were summing each other up. Wycliffe was amused, but though the two men had something in common, they were very different. Curtis was shrewd and subtle but essentially gentle, whereas in Marsden one sensed a potentiality for violence.

Marsden's attention came back to Wycliffe. 'You must think this is serious; a chief super on the job already.'

'Not necessarily. I happen to be involved because I'm staying with the Bishops over Christmas.'

Marsden grinned. 'Ah, the Bishops! God bless their little grey souls.' He took a cigarette pack from his pocket and lit one. Despite his bulk there was no clumsiness; he was as delicate and precise in his movements as a fastidious girl. 'I spoke to Fran after the church do last night. But the village K.G.B. will have told you that; it's probably why you're here.'

'Did she say why she didn't stay for the vicar's little party?'

'She said she couldn't face the vicar's sausage rolls.'

'How did you come to be talking to her?'

'Well, I saw her standing on the pavement like she was waiting for somebody. I told her I'd enjoyed the play and we chatted for a minute or two. I thought she was probably waiting for the Bateman boy to take her home the long way round. I believe that sort of thing is still done.'

Curtis said: 'Was she carrying anything?'

Marsden looked at Curtis with a speculative gaze. 'Ah! The monkey as well as the organ grinder. Yes, she was; a little holdall. "What did she have in it?" you say. And I say: "I do not know. I did not ask."'

Wycliffe said: 'I believe Francine sometimes comes here to your cottage.'

'True!'

'You are on friendly terms with her?'

'I am. She's a very intelligent girl, bored to the

eyeballs most of the time by the people she has to cope with. Me too, when I was a boy.'

'She comes here regularly?'

'She does, but I don't screw her if that's what you're asking.'

'Was the young woman who lives with you here last night?'

'No, the young woman who lives with me was not here last night; she went home to mother for Christmas.'

Curtis asked: 'Is she coming back?'

'I never ask women if they're coming back; it makes 'em think they're important. But she left her clobber here so I suppose she will.'

With an irritable movement Marsden threw the remains of his cigarette into the fire and got to his feet. 'I'll show you something. Come with me.'

He crossed the room, led them through a curtained doorway in the end wall, and switched on a strip-light which flickered into life. A large, bare room with a sloping roof on which the rain was pattering.

'My studio.'

It was very cold.

A couple of easels, a trolley painting-table, canvases stacked against the walls, a random assemblage of possible props, and the all-pervading smell of oil paint.

'Over here!'

Another strip-light. 'These things are supposed to give a north light, so that I can paint at night. No good! They're all wrong in the bloody yellows. Still, they're the best you can buy.

'Now look at this.' He lifted a cloth from a canvas on the second easel. 'There's our Fran for you. Stand back! You're not looking for the sodding signature.'

Wycliffe stood back and was impressed. A study in blues and greys and greens and purples with just a flush of pink in the flesh tones. The girl wore a flowered wrap, one breast exposed, and she looked at herself in a mirror.

51

Marsden said: 'She's not seeing herself; she's catching a glimpse of the promised land and she's not sure that she's going to like it. She's on the threshold. In another week, another month, perhaps a little longer, she'll have crossed over, she'll be a woman, then nobody will ever see that look again. But there it is on canvas; caught like a butterfly pinned out in a box. For good!' Marsden sighed. 'To do that you have to be a painter, and a bloody good one!'

Curtis said: 'It's a nice picture.'

Marsden turned to Wycliffe. 'Now you've seen that, do you think I screwed her – or, for that matter, that anybody else did? I could have; she's ready for it, and I'd have been a damn sight better for her than some sweaty youth, all elbows and acne who doesn't know what he's about. But I didn't.'

He continued to look at his picture. 'She'd hold that pose, with rests, for two hours without moving a muscle, and do you know what she'd say at the end of it?'

'I've no idea.'

'She'd say: "That's eight quid you owe me."'

'You paid her?'

'Of course I paid her; well above the going rate. She wouldn't have sat for me otherwise. She's not stupid.'

'How many times did she sit for you?'

'God knows! Seven or eight; you'll have to ask my secretary.'

He shepherded them back to the living-room, sat in his chair, and lit another cigarette. 'Now we know where we stand I've made up my mind to pass on one or two things I gathered from Fran.' He looked at Wycliffe. 'Of course, you know about papa Lemarque?'

'What about him?'

'That he's been in jug and only recently come out.'

'Go on.'

'It seems that Francine was very much looking forward to him coming home. You know how girls can get a fix on father; well, I won't say it went as far as that but,

52

after the best part of two years living with mother, I think she was counting on it all coming right when dad came back. It hasn't.'

'What was wrong, living with mother?'

Marsden pouted his thick lips. 'I'm not her confessor. She talks sometimes while I'm working and mostly I don't even answer, let alone ask questions, so I've no more than an impression.'

'And that is?'

'You've met the lady?'

'Mrs Lemarque? Briefly.'

'Then you can't fail to have noticed the Mona Lisa façade; the beautiful constipated nun look. One's natural reaction to that is: "Get behind it, mate, and you'll be all right." But what if there's no getting behind it? I know the score with her sort, it goes on and on until she gets clobbered and some poor bastard is carried away screaming: "There's nothing there! It was only a bloody record!"'

'Is that an expert assessment of why Francine has gone away?'

Marsden laughed. 'It's what you like to make it, mate. Now, if you don't mind, I was listening to some music and getting pissed ready for Christmas.'

'Benny Goodman,' Curtis said.

Marsden gave him a sour look. 'Who's a clever boy, then? I'll tell you something: when you pass this cottage you're just as likely to hear Bach or boogie-woogie.'

Outside, Curtis said: 'That gorilla isn't altogether stupid; I'll give him that.'

Wycliffe grumbled, 'Everybody seems anxious to talk about the mother rather than the girl. But it looks as though you were right. A planned get-away and she probably isn't short of money. It seems that somebody was due to pick her up in a car, so before we enlist the media with the "Have you seen?" bit we ought to really get down to finding who it was. There must have been quite a few people about, collecting their cars after the play. Only a fraction of the audience stayed for the sausage rolls but, according to the vicar, people came from all over this part of the county so you need to rope in other sections and get more men on the job. I'll speak to Division.'

Curtis said: 'I'll run you back to Mynhager, sir.'

'No need; I'll walk. I can do with the fresh air.'

'It's dark and it's damp, sir.'

'I'll survive.'

When Curtis drove off in the direction of the village the intensity of the darkness took Wycliffe by surprise. He set out with the fine rain in his face, picking his way with care, but soon the vague outlines of the landscape materialized out of the night and he walked with more confidence. The only light he could see came from across the valley, a dimly glowing orange rectangle, the window of the Lemarques' living-room. It happened that as he watched, their front door opened, illuminating a second rectangle; a figure appeared briefly in the light then the door closed again. Someone had come out of the house, someone with a torch; he could see the wavering pin-point of light as, whoever it was, descended the steps.

A few minutes later he rounded the bend which brought him in sight of the lights of Mynhager. Suddenly the sea sounded much louder and at intervals the low cloud was lit by diffused flashes from the lighthouse down the coast.

The meal over, they moved into the drawing-room. The wind had risen and despite the thick walls and heavy velvet curtains they could hear the waves breaking over the rocks and surging into the cove.

Joseph said: 'It's going to blow tonight.'

Time for party games.

Wycliffe sat in one of the big armchairs and his gaze ranged over the assembled Bishops and their distaff

54

branch, the Batemans. He was bored and he amused himself by trying to sum them up. Joseph, head of the clan, naturally domineering, presumed on the privileges of old-age to be caustic and sometimes cruel. A widower. Presumably the young woman in the only portrait amongst the pictures had been his wife. Ernest, over-dutiful son, suffered like his prototype in the parable. No fatted calf for Ernest. And the sisters? Virginia: unmarried, but still eligible if she got a move on: intelligent, good to look at, though spoiled at the moment by a too fussy hair-do and spectacles with shiny rims that were too large for her. Prim, in her royal-blue Jaeger frock, and probably in her panties, too. A hint of suppressed tension? Perhaps.

He wished that he could smoke but pride forbade it. Helen had said: 'Give it up in the New Year; you'll never hold out over Christmas.'

Then Caroline: plump but by no means cosy; her trouble was drink; more accurately, drink was the symptom of her trouble. Twenty-four hours at Mynhager was enough to convince anybody that her relationship with Gerald was not based on connubial felicity. Caroline, blatantly sexy, had opted to be separated from her husband for most of the year. There must be a story there. Wycliffe ruefully decided that he had missed his role in life; he should have been a housewife, peering through lace curtains. Are there any left?

Bateman was the odd man out. He lounged elegantly in one of the big chairs, smoking a cigarette, and staring at the ceiling but very far from being relaxed. No one could fail to be aware of his isolation, even from his son. It occurred to Wycliffe that Gerald had not yet subjected him to the threatened interrogation and he wondered why. They had scarcely exchanged half-a-dozen words.

Virginia, anxious to promote the party spirit, asked: 'What shall we play?'

Paul said: 'Let's play Who Am I?' The boy looked very

pale but he was behaving normally; keeping a stiff upper lip.

Who Am I? turned out to be a version of Twenty Questions in which one of them assumed the identify of a famous personage, living or dead, and the others had to discover that identity in not more than twenty questions.

Ernest, the first victim, was unmasked as Oscar Wilde by the sixteenth question. Virginia followed, and beat the field as Lady Astor.

Aunt Stella said: 'I knew Nancy Astor; we were invited to Cliveden several times. I always felt sorry for poor Waldorf, he was such a kindly man and Nancy was a dragon!'

Then it was Gerald's turn.

Joseph had been taking a lively part in the questioning; now he said: 'I'm enjoying this! Psychological striptease! Who would have thought poor old Ernest had tendencies or that Vee's frustrations were political? Your turn now, Gerry, and you'd better watch your step, you're treading on eggs! What about Churchill, or Ramsey Mac? Or go the whole hog with Talleyrand, he turned his coat so often that nobody knew for certain whose side he was on.'

Some years earlier Gerald had crossed the floor of the House and kept his seat.

Virginia and Ernest ignored their father but Gerald became very tense. In a manner far from his usual self-assured benevolence he said: 'I thought this was a game; but if you intend to use it as an occasion to work off some of your mischievous witticisms I am sure that you will manage just as well without me!' With that, Gerald got up and walked out, closing the door carefully behind him.

Joseph had cut too deep and he felt foolish. In the silence he said: 'What's the matter with him?'

Caroline muttered: 'Stupid bastard!'

Very slowly the party recovered its equanimity and its momentum. At ten o'clock Wycliffe was called to the telephone.

Curtis reporting: 'Some progress, sir. A witness says she saw the girl who took the part of the Virgin, getting into a car near the church at about nine-fifteen. She couldn't say what make the car was and she couldn't see its colour because the light was poor, but she thought it could have been red. She thought it looked a bit like a sports car, but old. She couldn't see who was driving.'

'Anything else?'

'Yes, and it ties up. One of my chaps unearthed the girl's form teacher. She says that at least twice in the last few days of term Francine didn't catch the school bus home; she was picked up by somebody in a red car. She only saw the car from a distance and couldn't see who was driving, but she had heard that Francine's father was back home and assumed that he was calling for her but didn't like to come too near the school.'

'You may have a good lead there.'

Back in the drawing-room they were passing round refreshments, little morsels on sticks and balanced on biscuits. Surely Christmas must be the feast of gluttony. Then more games, more drinks. At a little before midnight Gerald came back and resumed his seat as though nothing had happened. Glasses were filled with Joseph's '55 port then, with the radio switched on, they waited for the time signal. At midnight precisely they drank a toast 'To Christmas, friends and family!'

Even then Joseph had the last word: '"And God bless us all! said Tiny Tim."'

Came the presents; distributed by Paul, the youngest member of the party; the great business of unwrapping, the floor littered with pretty Christmas paper; the cries of surprise and delight; the somewhat effusive expressions of gratitude; and the moments of secret misgiving when one wonders whether one's own contributions have matched the general level, appearing neither ostentatious nor mean.

And finally, at about one o'clock, up the stairs to bed. By this time the gale was blowing in mighty gusts so that the old house shuddered. A single gust might last for fifteen or twenty seconds, followed by an abrupt and uneasy calm, an interval while the wind seemed to gather force for its next assault. Occasionally the electric lights flickered and Wycliffe wondered what it must have been like when the only lighting came from candles and oil lamps.

In his bedroom Wycliffe drew back the curtains but dared not open the windows. The roar of the sea and wind merged in a fury and it was impossible to decide whether the water streaming down the window panes came from rain or from spray. Through the watery curtain he looked down on the seething whiteness of breakers racing into the cove. He listened, and thought he could hear the great boulders grinding together, underscoring the rest of the wild orchestration.

In 120 years the house must have come through worse.

He thought about the Bishops. They had been pleasant enough, almost embarrassingly attentive, thoughtful and generous with their presents. Leaving aside the old man's mischievous wit, their hospitality could hardly be faulted. But he felt uncomfortable; there was an atmosphere: they all seemed edgy and preoccupied. They were going ahead with the business of entertaining him and with the rituals of Christmas but he had the impression that their thoughts were on something quite different.

Francine Lemarque?

Perhaps. It was natural that they should be concerned about the girl but there seemed to be more to it than that.

His thinking was muzzy; he had had rather too much to drink. He prepared for bed and got between the sheets.

Despite the pandemonium outside he could hear a woman's voice in the next room: Caroline, quarrelling with her husband. A happy Christmas.

He switched off the bedside lamp and snuggled down, thinking vaguely of Helen and tropical nights.

CHAPTER FOUR

He slept well considering the violence of the storm. Now and then, when rain or spray lashed against the windows with malevolent force he would mutter sleepily to himself, but he had gone to bed slightly tipsy, enough to feel superior to the elements.

He was up by eight-thirty; the worst seemed to be over though the wind blew at storm force and from time to time squalls of drenching rain swept in from the sea. The sky was a low canopy of driven clouds and the sea was lashed to foam for as far as the eye could see. The terrace was drenched by every wave and spume slid down the window panes.

Breakfast was a scratch affair, with Virginia and Ada in the kitchen handing out coffee and toast to anyone who turned up. Ernest was there, eating toast with so much butter on it that his moustache dripped and made Wycliffe feel slightly embarrassed. Joseph, Gerald, and Paul did not appear but to Wycliffe's astonishment, Caroline was in the drawing-room playing Rachmaninov with tremendous zest in the fortissimo passages. The morning after? A release from frustration? Or a celebration of victory? Strange woman!

Ernest said: 'Carrie is good, don't you think? She was at the Royal College and she did a year in Paris. She could have made a career but she said she'd been away from home long enough, so that was that. A real Cornish girl, our Carrie!'

Wycliffe asked: 'Have you heard from the Lemarques this morning?'

'No, I haven't. I'll telephone presently if the lines aren't down.'

A few minutes later Curtis came through. 'Not too early for you, I hope, sir? A happy Christmas! I'm speaking from home, as you can probably hear.'

Thumps, squeals and shrieks in the background from Curtis's grandchildren.

'Anything fresh?'

'We've traced the red car, sir, a 1975 Triumph belonging to a young layabout called Pellowe – Timothy Pellowe. His father is a builder in a small way in St Buryan.'

'How young is young?'

'Oh, he's not exactly a boy, he's nineteen, rising twenty. The perpetual student type who never studies anything. He got chucked out of university last July for failing his exams and he's been bumming around ever since, coming home to mum and dad when times are hard but taking off into the wide blue yonder when it suits him. Like now. This time he's been home since early December.'

'Anything known?'

'No, he hasn't got form but, from what I hear, he's not the sort I'd want a daughter of mine running off with.'

'His parents haven't any idea where he might be?'

'Not a clue; nor has anybody else we've talked to so far. All he said was that he'd probably be back in a few days.'

'Of course you must do this through Division, but I want all you've got on the couple and the car put on the telex. At the same time they might try to find somebody in the TV and radio newsrooms who stays awake over Christmas and see if we can get a mention.'

Ernest could not get through to the Lemarques. 'Their line is dead; it's usually like this after a blow; a toss-up who gets cut off and who doesn't. I'll take a walk over there directly.'

Wycliffe said: 'I thought of going over myself.' He contrived without being offensive to convey the message that he wanted to go alone.

'Oh! In that case . . . ' After a pause Ernest went on: 'This young fellow she's gone off with; they must have planned it.'

'Of course.'

'Then wouldn't you have expected her to leave a note of some sort?'

'Perhaps she did.' Wycliffe went on quickly: 'I don't know if you would care to give Paul the latest news – such as it is.'

Perversity decided him to walk, despite the weather. He put on his heavy waterproof and a matching peaked cap which, according to Helen, made him look like Our Man in Berlin. It was not actually raining but mist and spray mingled in the rampageous air and he was driven along the dirt road by the force of the wind. He reached the painter's cottage where there was no sign of life. Marsden was probably sleeping it off. He turned down the footpath to the bridge, but the bridge, a ramshackle affair at best, had collapsed and been swept away by the stream, now a miniature torrent of brown water. He would have to walk to the village and down the old mine track on the other side.

He was out of humour with himself, low on Christmas spirit, and disgruntled with his job. Why was he getting into this anyway? A missing girl, a juvenile who had run away with a boy three or four years older. Teenagers went missing every day; and every day a few more took to glue sniffing; smoking pot; swallowing, sniffing or injecting themselves with daydreams which turned into nightmares. And the police were all but helpless. Every day young people (older ones too) robbed or mugged or raped or murdered, and many chief constables would be over the moon if their detection rate came within shouting distance of 50 per cent. Add to this strikes, violence on the picket lines, violence at football matches, violence at demonstrations for and against almost everything.

He was Canute, striving to halt the tide; Quixote, tilting at windmills; better still, that Greek chap, Sisyphus, condemned through all eternity to roll a stone uphill so that it could roll down again.

Sensible people raised the drawbridge, kept their fingers crossed, and learned Russian. But here he was, getting wet to bring to the Lemarques news of their daughter's stupidity. Curtis could and would have done all that was needed. The truth was that he felt uneasy. During the night he had recalled an incident that had occurred on his way back from the painter's cottage in the dark. The orange rectangle of the Lemarques' window, the opening and closing of their door, and the erratic movements of a flashlight held in someone's hand. It was absurd, but that trivial sequence of events had acquired a dramatic significance in his mind.

In the village street a little boy was pedalling furiously around on a brand new 'Chopper' bicycle, oblivious of the weather, imagining himself on a Yamaha or a Honda. Outside two or three of the houses cars were unloading guests laden with parcels; there were Christmas trees with lights in several windows and through some he could see the flickering glow of a television set. The Tributers was not yet open but there were a few cars parked by the church and he could hear the sound of the organ.

He had trouble finding the alley which led to the mine track but came upon it at last between the Mechanics' Institute (1853), and a terrace of cottages. In places it was rough going with puddles of peaty water which could only be avoided by taking to the heather, and now the wind was in his face. Head down, he fought against it and reached the cottage at last. There was no van parked at the bottom of the steps and he was wondering if they had gone out when he saw that the front door was open. From that moment he had no doubt that his instinct had been right.

He climbed the steps. The door was wide open and the drab carpet and mats in the little passage were sodden with blown rain. A flimsy plant-stand had been overturned, perhaps by the wind, so that plant and pot had parted company and there was soil strewn over the floor.

He was picking his way through to the living-room when he heard a sound and he called out: 'Is anyone there?'

Heavy footsteps, and Marsden appeared in the door-way of the living-room. He looked at Wycliffe in a bemused, uncomprehending way and for a moment Wycliffe thought he was drunk. He was wearing slacks that were wet below the knees and a roll-neck pullover stained with paint and grime; his black curls had been flattened by the rain and there were droplets of moisture caught in his moustache.

Wycliffe said: 'What are you doing here?'

The painter supported himself against the doorpost and spoke as though he were short of breath. 'I saw from my place that the door was open when I got up this morning . . . Half-an-hour later it was still open and I wondered if there was something wrong. Lemarque's van wasn't there and I thought they might have gone off and not shut the door properly . . . The bridge was down so I had to walk round.' He gestured weakly. 'There seemed to be nobody here and it was obvious the door had been open for a long time. I couldn't under-stand it so I came in to look round . . . Of course, I found her.'

'Francine?' Wycliffe's voice was sharp.

'Not Francine, Jane. She's up in the bedroom, and she's dead.'

'Stay where you are!'

Wycliffe went up the stairs. At the top was a landing

with three doors opening off. The room in front of him was Francine's, he could see the single bed and the pop-star posters on the wall. Another door opened into a tiny bathroom with a loo. He turned to the third door; it was almost closed and he pushed it open. There were yellow curtains drawn over the tiny window and a pale, jaundiced light reached into the room from the grey world outside. It was a moment before his eyes became adjusted to the gloom. A double bed took up most of the space and the bed was made up, though untidily, as if someone had been lying across it.

Then he saw her, on the floor, her body was wedged between the bed and the dressing table. She was wearing the drab woollen two-piece he had seen her in the day before. He bent over her. In order to do so he had to sprawl across the bed. She was lying on her side but her head was twisted so that he could see her face. The pale, serene features had been grossly mutilated by a bullet leaving her skull; a bullet which must have made its entry through the back of the head or the neck. He reached down and tried to raise her hand. Jane Lemarque was dead and she had been dead for several hours.

He got to his feet and looked at his watch. Ten thirty-five.

'At ten thirty-five on the morning of December 25th I entered the larger of the two bedrooms and found the deceased lying on the floor between the bed and dressing table. She appeared to be fully clothed. She was in such a position that I was able to see the injury to the upper part of her face which I took to be the wound of exit of a bullet fired from behind. I satisfied myself that life was extinct . . .'

Accustomed to such scenes, his reactions were professional, but he had never become hardened. He was still deeply shocked by violent death; by the senseless destruction of a web of consciousness which reached back to the womb.

Marsden mustn't be left downstairs alone. What the

hell had he been doing in the living-room anyway? And he was not wearing a coat or mackintosh, only a pullover and slacks . . . But Jane Lemarque had been dead for many hours.

Downstairs, Marsden was still standing in the doorway of the living-room as though dazed.

'You saw her?'

He couldn't keep the man standing there, he was liable to fall down but if he let him go back into the living-room the scene-of-crime chaps would go berserk.

'You can sit on the stairs.'

Marsden lowered his bulk on to the second stair and sat with his hands on his knees. His pullover was quite dry.

'Where's your coat?'

Marsden pointed to the living-room. 'In there.' He passed a hand over his forehead. 'Christ! I hardly know what I'm doing. I went in there to telephone but the bloody wires had been cut . . . I was going to call your lot and I thought the quickest way would be to twist the ends together.' He held out his right hand and opened it. He had been gripping a small penknife with an open blade which had cut into the flesh and brought blood.

'I was stripping the wires when you came.'

'And your coat?'

He shifted irritably. 'I slipped the bloody thing off because it was in the way. Why keep on about it?'

It sounded feasible.

'You stay where you are.'

Wycliffe went into the living-room and to the telephone. The wires had been cut near the instrument and the ends were bared. Marsden's coat – stained and worn suede with lambswool facings – lay in a heap on the floor.

He twisted the wires together as best he could and it worked. He made the routine calls. To Division: Locate Detective Sergeant Curtis; send a patrol car, a couple of uniformed men, and a police surgeon; notify the coroner. Then he spoke to his own office. That Christmas morning the duty strength at C.I.D. headquarters was a detective sergeant and two constables, all three engaged in the perilous cut and thrust of gin rummy. Along with a lot of other people they were about to have their simple pleasures brutally cut short.

Wycliffe's deputy, Chief Inspector John Scales, was located at the home of a friend and from now on the wheels would begin to turn. The pathologist would be notified, a mobile incident post would be sent to Mulfra and preparations put in hand to get a team on the road. The leader of the team: Detective Inspector Kersey. In the interests of promotion Kersey had served his time in the wilderness, now he was returning to the fold and no one was more pleased than Wycliffe.

He rejoined Marsden.

Marsden had a cigarette going and he had recovered something of his usual poise. 'So that's how it's done.'

Wycliffe said: 'You will be required to make a statement later but I am going to ask you a few questions.'

'Ask away.'

'Yesterday morning I saw an old grey Escort van parked outside here. Is it theirs?'

'I suppose so; it turned up shortly after he came out of jail.'

'You knew Lemarque before he went to prison?'

Marsden looked around for somewhere to dispose of the butt-end of his cigarette then pitched it through the open doorway. 'I knew him by sight and to pass the time of day. They came down quite often and stayed at the cottage for a weekend; longer, sometimes. He had money and a Jag then.' Marsden grinned in something like his old style. 'But no particular interest in impoverished genius, women, or booze, so our paths didn't cross.'

'While Lemarque was in jail, did his wife associate with other men?'

'How the hell should I know?'

67

'You were recommended to me as an expert on such matters.'

A short laugh. 'I'm flattered. But I'm no expert where that lady is concerned. She strikes me as the sort who needs a man about as much as I need a hole in the head but you never can tell; impressions can be deceptive.' He broke off. 'Christ! It's hard to remember that she's up there, poor little cow! Was that a shotgun wound?'

'No. What time did you get up this morning?'

Marsden passed a hand over his hair and looked at it foolishly when he realized that it was wet. 'I shall catch my death over this, I've got a weak chest. My mother used to say, "Keep your head, your feet and your bum dry and you'll be all right." It must've been about nine.'

'And the van was already gone?'

'Yes.'

'When did you last see Lemarque?'

The painter grimaced. 'I haven't a clue.'

'His van?'

'You'll think I spend my time looking out of the bloody window like the old bags in the village, but it happens I did see the van yesterday afternoon, at about half-two, perhaps earlier, being driven along the track towards the village. I suppose Lemarque was driving. I don't think Jane can – could.' He hesitated. 'You think he killed her?'

Wycliffe said, 'Do you? Or do you have good reason to know that he didn't?'

The painter shook his head. 'My God! This should teach me not to play the good Samaritan. In future, Marsden, you'll keep your head down, and your eyes shut. I don't know whether Lemarque killed his wife but it wouldn't surprise me; not that I know anything about Lemarque but some women are born victims and she was one.'

On the face of it the shooting had taken place sometime the previous evening or early in the night. It had the marks of a domestic crime; no evidence of

68

burglary (was there anything to take?), apparently no sexual overtones; and no husband available for comment. Unless he had a cast-iron alibi it looked as though the case would be as good as over when Lemarque was brought in. And that shouldn't be difficult.

It would be simple to put Lemarque and his van on the telex. As an ex-con Lemarque would be on record and details of the van should be available through Vehicle Registration. But he needed to get Marsden off his hands first. He didn't want an audience.

The sound of a car grinding along the track. Wycliffe went to the door. Two coppers in a patrol car, their meditations on the Nativity in some quiet lay-by rudely interrupted. Curtis came hard on their heels. Wycliffe put him in the picture.

Curtis's button-eyes looked at Wycliffe with concern. 'Do you think this has anything to do with the girl?'

'How do I know? But it makes it all the more important to find her.' He gave Curtis detailed instructions to put Lemarque and his van on the telex, then he called Marsden over. 'Mr Marsden will go with you to make his statement.'

Marsden gave him a sour look. 'And when will Mr Marsden get back to feed his cat and perform other necessary domestic chores?'

'That depends on Mr Marsden.'

'I suppose I can take my coat?'

'Not for the moment; anyway, there's central heating in the nick.'

As Curtis was leaving with Marsden, two uniformed men arrived in a Panda Car with a detective sergeant from Division.

It would be the better part of two hours before the pathologist or the headquarters circus could arrive so he left the detective sergeant in charge and got one of the patrolmen to drive him back to Mynhager. The car jolted over the bumpy track and splashed through the pools while the uniformed driver sat beside him, stiff and silent as though stuffed. It was raining hard again; the village street streamed with water, gleaming darkly, and was utterly deserted. There were cars outside The Tributers, the bar was brightly lit, and they caught a snatch of song as they passed. Turning off down the road to Mynhager they met the full force of the wind with the rain driving straight off the sea.

'Are you due off at two?'

'With a bit of luck, sir, I'll be able to spend some time with the kids.'

'Have a good day, what's left of it.'

Wycliffe was thinking of Francine's disappearance and of her mother's murder. A connection? He believed in coincidence as he believed in Sants Claus but coincidences do happen. Arthur Koestler wrote a book about them. A girl goes missing on the night before Christmas Eve, and on Christmas morning her mother is found, shot dead. And her father? Wycliffe was relieved that Francine had been seen getting into the red car, otherwise the prospect might have seemed even more sinister.

But his immediate problem was with the Bishops. The Bishops, the Batemans and the Lemarques had been closely associated for years and the Lemarques had been almost members of the family. Not any more. After Bateman pulled out of the partnership and Lemarque got the bit between his teeth to end up in jail, the situation had changed.

Policemen are fated to be an embarrassment to their friends and to themselves. Accept a lift in a friend's car and he thinks you are checking his tax disc, his speed and his braking. Jane Lemarque had been murdered and now questions would be asked, some of them relevant, others not. But the people questioned would feel disturbed and possibly threatened, and the Bishops and Batemans were bound to be in the forefront. Even if it turned out that Lemarque had killed his wife, the police would need to know why, and they would look to Mynhager for at least part of the answer.

Ergo: it was impossible for him to continue as a guest in the house.

Ernest, his glasses pushed up on to his forehead, was sitting at a table looking down a binocular microscope at a minute insect impaled on a pin. On the table was a shallow, cork-lined drawer with its glass cover lying beside it. In the drawer, other flies, similarly impaled, were lined up like guardsmen, each with a tiny cardboard label. A cabinet under the window held at least a score of such drawers.

'I hope I'm not disturbing you.'

Ernest swivelled his chair away from the table. 'My dear Charles! I'm merely filling in time until lunch looking at a few flies I took yesterday.'

His 'den' was a little room sandwiched between dining-room and drawing-room. The window, covered with a grubby net curtain, looked out on the courtyard at the back of the house.

'Any news of Francine?'

'Not of Francine but I'm afraid there's very bad news of the Lemarques.'

'Indeed?' A look of concern.

'Jane has been shot; when I saw her earlier this morning she had been dead for several hours at least.'

Ernest's features expressed total incredulity. 'Shot? You mean she's killed herself?'

Wycliffe shook his head. 'It wasn't suicide, it was murder.'

'And Alain?' The question seemed to be forced from him.

'Lemarque and his van are missing.'

'Oh God!' He got up from his chair and went to the window. 'Are you suggesting that he killed his wife — murdered her?'

71

'All I can say is that Jane Lemarque has been murdered and that her husband is missing. You know them better than I do. Is it credible that he murdered her? Is he a violent man? Do you know of any motive he may have had or thought he had?'

An electric clock on the wall above the table flicked the seconds away. Ernest had his back to the room; he was wearing a woolly cardigan which hung limply from his thin shoulders and his whole body seemed to droop. He looked like an old man. At last he turned away from the window. 'Alain is not a violent man, Charles, quite the contrary, and I'm sure that he was fond of Jane.' But he spoke without conviction. 'I don't know what to say. Is this anything to do with Francine running away?'

'I've no idea.'

Ernest said: 'I suppose you will be taking charge of the investigation? You don't need me to tell you that you are welcome to stay on here.'

'I'm very grateful but it wouldn't do at all. You must see that.'

Ernest looked at him in pained surprise. 'Surely, this isn't going to affect us – our relationship, I mean?'

'I'm afraid it's bound to do until the case is over. I have to go back to being a policeman. You're a lawyer, you know the score. How can I possibly conduct an investigation while remaining on intimate terms with a family so closely connected with the dead woman?'

Ernest slumped into his chair and swivelled listlessly to and fro. 'No, I suppose you are right, but I have to admit that it's a blow . . . What a Christmas Day this has turned out to be!'

Wycliffe was aware of the curious museum-like smell of the room, a blend of cork, naphthalene, old books, and preserving spirit. He had the odd notion that it was Ernest's main concern to arrest the passage of time, to hold on to the moment and preserve the status quo . . .

'So you are leaving us . . . You'll stay to lunch – you won't just walk out?' It was a plea.

'Of course I'll stay; and thank you.'

'Good! Just give me a few minutes to break the news to the others.'

In the dining-room everyone was subdued and Wycliffe felt like a leper though they seemed anxious to make it clear that his position was understood. Only Joseph and Aunt Stella were seated, Paul wasn't there, and the others stood about going through the motions of helping themselves to bits of chicken, slices of ham, and a variety of salads, all laid out on the table.

Virginia said: 'It's hardly credible! In less than forty-eight hours, the whole family . . . Just gone!'

Caroline picked at the chicken with her fork. 'I can't believe that Alain killed her. Jane was difficult, God knows, but she was the only one for him. I doubt if he ever looked at another woman.'

Joseph was helping himself from a bottle of hock. 'If I'd been married to Jane I can imagine a situation in which I might have strangled her, but shooting, that's another thing altogether. You have to have a gun, you have to load it, aim it, and pull the trigger. Premeditation.' The old man shook his head. 'But who else is there?'

Aunt Stella had seemed unaware of or indifferent to what had happened and what was being said; she had a plate of food and she was working through it. Then, abruptly, with perfect enunciation, she recited:

'"Lizzie Borden with an axe,
Hit her father forty whacks.
When she saw what she had done,
She hit her mother forty-one."'

A shocked silence, but the old lady was in no way subdued. She looked round at the family. 'What's the matter? All I'm saying is I would be more willing to believe it of the girl than of her father. We all know that

73

Alain Lemarque is a rogue but nothing will convince me that he is a murderer.'

Virginia was outraged. 'But that's monstrous, Aunt Stella! A terrible thing to say!'

Caroline turned on her sister. 'You've always defended Francine but there's something in what Aunt Stella says. I don't know whether Francine could or would have done it but I don't forget what she was like when she was here. Don't you remember when she smashed her mother's gold watch just because she was stopped from going on some trip? How old was she then . . . five? . . . six? No tears, no show of temper but straight up the stairs to her mother's dressing table. And that's not the only—'

'Stop it, Carrie!' Ernest's voice raised in real anger. 'There may be some excuse for Aunt Stella but there is none for the rest of us. We are turning a tragedy affecting our friends into poisonous gossip!'

Wycliffe noted the effect of this outburst on the others. Bateman nodded agreement. Old Joseph looked at his son with a faint smile on his lips. Caroline's expression was one of unbelief like a cat who has been bitten by a mouse. Stella remained unperturbed.

Lunch was over at last and Wycliffe went upstairs to do his packing. There was a knock on his bedroom door and Gerald Bateman came in, a diffident and confiding Bateman.

'I hope I'm not intruding but I felt that I must speak to you before you cease to be a guest and become a policeman.' A thin smile. 'You can imagine how I feel. I've known Alain and Jane for twenty years. Alain and I not only worked together but we shared a good deal of our social life both here and in London. The differences I had with Alain which ended our partnership and led eventually to his trouble with the law in no way diminished my affection and respect for them both. We continued friends.'

'Have you seen anything of him since you've been home this time?'

'I called there; it was my first chance following his release.'

'How did you find him?'

The great man considered. 'I found him changed but what could one expect?'

'Depressed?'

'Not depressed, subdued.' He lowered his voice. 'As a matter of fact he was sounding me out about putting up capital for a scheme he had in mind. He wasn't ready to discuss it in any detail but I gathered that it was local and concerned with tourism. More than that he was not prepared to say at this stage.'

'Were you able to give him any encouragement?'

'Yes, I was, and not only out of a desire to help an old friend. Alain is a first-rate businessman and, with certain safeguards, I would be fully prepared to back a scheme he believed to be sound. Of course, a partnership would hardly be practicable in the new circumstances but I think he has it in mind that I should provide the capital and he would run the business for a share in the profits.'

Wycliffe stooped to fasten his suitcase. Politicians are by nature devious and he was wondering about the real purpose of Bateman's confidences. However, he rarely tried to meet guile with subtlety. The suitcase secured, he straightened up, put on his ruminating-cow look, and asked: 'Why are you telling me all this?'

By the same token Bateman was far too old a hand to be disconcerted. 'Because I want you to know that whatever precipitated this tragedy it was not, I think, a feeling of hopelessness about the future.'

Wycliffe thought, he wants me to believe that Lemarque murdered his wife and he may well be right. He said: 'Paul wasn't at lunch; if he's around I would like a word with him before I leave.'

No doubt Bateman had survived many more devastating snubs and he took this one in his stride. 'There is just one other matter: I hope you won't be influenced by the talk during lunch. I'm afraid my wife is in the habit of making outrageous remarks, just to shock. The family take no notice, but to a stranger . . . ' A bleak smile. 'As for Aunt Stella's nonsense! . . . '

Wycliffe said: 'I expect I shall hear a great deal of nonsense during the next few days.'

Bateman nodded. 'You reassure me. If you want Paul you will almost certainly find him in his workshop. It's his refuge in time of trouble. The old wash-house, I'll show you.'

They had to go through the kitchen where Ada was washing dishes, then through an empty cavernous room with whitewashed walls and a slate floor.

'Here we are!' Bateman pushed open another door and they were in a businesslike workshop. There was a carpenter's bench, woodworking tools neatly arranged in racks, and the delectable blended smells of resin and sawdust. Paul was there, bending over what looked like a bench-end, supported on trestles.

'Paul is carving new ends for some of the pews in the church . . . I'll leave you to it.' Bateman, being discreet.

Paul straightened. He was holding a gouge and he was engaged in carving a new bench-end which had already been shaped. The motif was a herring-gull, about to touch down on the water. It was simple and incisive, fitting the rectangular space. There were three more ends lying against one of the walls, carved with a crab, a lobster, and a St Ives gig.

'I came here because I couldn't think of anything else to do.' He stood, taller than Wycliffe, pale-faced, diffident, and slightly embarrassed. 'It's only a hobby for the holidays.'

'But they will be used, surely?'

'Well, yes. The Vicar thinks the Victorian bench-ends are dull; there are only two survivors of the original sixteenth-century ones and he feels that we could liven some of the rest up a bit. Uncle Ernest said he would pay for the wood and the fitting if I carved them.' He paused awkwardly. 'I don't suppose there's any news of Francine?'

'I'm sorry, no. I came here because I thought you might help me. I'm trying to find out what things were like in the Lemarque household before and after Mr Lemarque came out of prison . . . You realize, Paul, that the time has gone for any kind of reticence.'

The boy nodded. 'I see that, but there's very little I can tell you. Francine never talks much about her home. I don't think she got on very well with her mother and sometimes she seemed quite rude to her, but I think Mrs Lemarque used to exasperate Francine by always being . . .'

'Being what?'

'I don't know; sort of miserable, I suppose, and resigned to being miserable. I think that is what upset Francine.'

'What was Francine's attitude to her father?'

'She seemed to look forward to him coming home.'

'And was she disappointed?'

He hesitated. 'I think she was.'

'Have you any idea why?'

He looked worried. 'It's very difficult to say, but Mr Lemarque had changed; I could see that. He was very quiet and he seemed depressed. He didn't have a lot to say before, but he used to be cheerful, he would tease people, especially Francine, and they used to laugh together.'

'Have there been quarrels since he came home?'

'I don't know; I only know that Francine was even more unhappy. Just a couple of days before she went away she said: "There's one thing you learn from parents – never get married."'

Wycliffe said: 'You are obviously very fond of Francine and you will not want to betray her confidences but in the new circumstances you must realize that you can help best by being completely frank. Has Francine said anything to you recently which, with hindsight, might throw any light on what has happened?'

Paul stood, testing the edge of the gouge with his thumb. 'I can't think of anything. I mean, she doesn't

77

confide in me much . . . The only thing she said recently which I didn't understand was something about me knowing more about her . . . '

'What exactly did she say?'

'It was something like: "When you know more about me you won't want me".'

'There's more, isn't there?'

He coloured. 'I said that I wanted to spend my life getting to know her and she laughed. She said that it wouldn't take that long; that I might find out more than I wanted to know very soon.'

Why did Wycliffe at that moment feel that Paul would follow in his uncle's footsteps? A confirmed bachelor, never taking a firm grip, making the best of a life divided between his work and his hobbies: the legal practice, Mynhager, wood carving, the aunts . . .

Wycliffe said: 'Thanks; you've straightened out my ideas a bit. I'll let you know as soon as we hear any news of Francine.'

Paul turned to put the gouge he was holding back in the rack so that Wycliffe could not see his face. 'Did my father . . . ?'

'Yes?'

He shook his head. 'Sorry! It doesn't matter.'

'You missed lunch. See if Ada has any food left in the kitchen.'

The boy smiled. 'I might do that.'

Wycliffe's case was in the hall; someone had brought it down. Ernest and Virginia came out to see him off. Ernest said: 'I hope you'll come again, bring Helen, and stay longer.'

Ernest walked with him to the car. 'Carrie's tongue runs away with her. She really doesn't mean what she says. Alain, Jane and Francine were like members of the family and what has happened is a tragedy for all of us.'

CHAPTER FIVE

He drove back to the Lemarques' cottage. Still raining, and in an hour or so the gloom would merge with the dusk. In the village, at the turn-off to the mine track, a uniformed copper was poised to direct new arrivals and divert the inquisitive. When he saw Wycliffe's indicators flash he raised a minatory hand and came to the car window.

'Do you have business down there, sir?' Water dribbled off his flower-pot helmet as he stooped to speak.

'Chief Superintendent Wycliffe.'

'Sorry, sir! I didn't recognize you. You know where it is?'

'I don't think I shall miss it. Has anybody arrived?'

'The police surgeon has been and gone, sir; a head-quarters party is there, and Dr Franks, the pathologist, went down a couple of minutes ago.'

So far none of the locals seemed to have realized that anything was happening, but that would change; with more police activity than the village had seen since D.H. Lawrence and Frieda were chased out as suspected German spies during the First War.

Lined up along the track beyond the cottage were two police cars, a police Range Rover, and a lethal-looking James Bond vehicle which could only belong to Dr Franks, the pathologist.

Franks himself was standing just inside the front door of the cottage, spick and span in herring-bone tweed with a striped shirt and club tie.

'Hullo, Charles! Is this your idea of Christmas? Apparently the lady most concerned in all this is upstairs and Fox is up there with the photographer taking pictures while she's *in situ,* so to speak. Fox is a keen lad; he doesn't want me prodding her about until they've finished. What's it all about?'

'A shooting.'

'I know that, but why was she shot? A domestic tiff?'

'I've no idea.' Although they had worked together for years, Franks still irritated Wycliffe by his frivolous attitude in the face of death, with the effect that Wycliffe became morose and taciturn.

'I hear that you are staying down here.'

Wycliffe pointed across the valley. 'With the Bishops; he's a lawyer, you may know him.'

Franks grimaced. 'I do. Christmas with him must be as exciting as a Jewish funeral. And this place – fine in summer but now! You're a masochist, Charles! I hear Helen is in Kenya. Nights of tropical splendour and all that. Well, I suppose that's how you want it.'

'Ready for you, doctor.' Sergeant Fox, in charge of the scene-of-crime investigation and successor to the misanthropic Smith, now retired. This was Fox's first murder case since joining the squad. Seeing Wycliffe, he came downstairs and Franks went up. Fox was twenty-eight, thin with sandy-coloured hair and freckles; he had a prominent nose and a receding chin but contrived to look intelligent despite everything.

'I didn't know you were here, sir.' Fox was preoccupied, watching Franks as he climbed the stairs; he said wistfully: 'I wish Dr Franks would wear the correct gear.' Fox, himself, looked like a one-man decontamination squad. The idea was to minimize 'exchange' at the scene of crime, to ensure that traces left by the criminal were neither confused nor destroyed by the investigator. Wycliffe remembered a pathologist who scattered cigar ash over the scene of crime as a priest sprinkles holy water.

He was depressed by changes, they made him feel

old; like the reading glasses, tucked neatly in their case in his right-hand jacket pocket. He would bring them out only when absolutely necessary, and put them on with the surreptitious air of a man who is forced to zip up his flies in public.

The doldrums: a period after the discovery of a major crime during which resources are mobilized and the preliminary technical data are established. No point in rushing around in ever diminishing circles while this is going on.

Dr Franks came down the stairs. 'She's on the bed now, Charles. Move her when you like.'

'The van is on the way. What have you got for me?'

'Not much. She was shot with a large calibre bullet which your chaps will dig out of the walls or the woodwork. It must have played merry hell inside her head and neck. She's been dead between sixteen and twenty hours so she was shot between four and eight yesterday. No sign of other injuries that I can see; no indications of assault, sexual or otherwise, apart from the shooting. If there's any more to tell you, after I've had a chance to take a real look, I'll be in touch later today. Who's attending?'

'Inspector Trevena from Division is coming with the van.'

Franks stood at the top of the steps. It was quite dark now, every light in the little cottage was switched on and a weak orange glow reached out into the pit-like darkness of the valley. It had stopped raining but the air was full of moisture and tangy with salt. The gale had blown itself out but the continuous muffled roar of the sea seemed sometimes very close, sometimes distant.

He held out his hand. 'I'll be off then. What a way to spend Christmas!'

A moment or two later, the roar of his car engine, two great shafts of light cleaving the valley, a skidding of tyres, and he was away.

Not robbery, not a sex crime; just a housewife shot

with a heavy calibre gun. Probably she had been threatened downstairs and, terrified, she had retreated up the stairs with some idea of protecting herself, only to be ruthlessly cornered and shot. Like an execution.

By her husband? Caroline Bateman hadn't thought so. 'She was the only one for him. I doubt if he ever looked at another woman.' And Wycliffe suspected that Caroline understood these things. But a passionate quarrel, perhaps over Francine running away? A quarrel which suddenly flared into uncontrollable violence? Joseph had pointed out the snags there. 'You have to have the gun . . . load it, aim it, and pull the trigger.' It becomes in some degree a premeditated act. But what other possibilities were there? Francine? There were cases on record of young girls murdering their parents, but he couldn't take the possibility seriously here. Anyway, what had happened to Lemarque? There remained the ubiquitous outsider . . .

His instinct was to wander around the little house, soaking up the atmosphere, getting the feel of how it had been lived in, but if he did this before the scene-of-crime boys had finished he would be unpopular with Fox. Criminal investigation, like other social studies, was struggling to qualify as a science, to join the other sacred cows and become a private stamping ground for experts. Wycliffe sympathized to some extent with the ineffable Poirot and his little grey cells. 'It is the psychology, *mon ami!*' In particular he agreed with the Belgian that a clue two-foot long is in no way inferior to one that must be sought under a microscope.

He growled like an irritated grizzly, giving vent to a vague and disquieting awareness that he was becoming increasingly out of step with the way things were going in his profession. He climbed the stairs. Fox, as though activated by a spring, came out from the main bedroom. 'You wanted me, sir?'

'No.'

'We've got the bullet and cartridge-case. It's a nine-millimetre.' Good dog, waiting to be patted.

A cold look. 'You know what to do, I suppose?' Wycliffe, like Talleyrand, distrusted enthusiasm: Above all, gentlemen, not the slightest zeal.

He followed Fox into the bedroom. The room looked as though it had been got ready for the removal men; the bed was dismantled, the bedding neatly folded; drawers were removed and the furniture pulled as far as possible away from the walls.

'Found anything?'

Fox pointed to the dressing table. Laid out on the top were a number of documents and papers beside an old-fashioned cash box with a brass handle. 'The papers were in the box and the box was in one of the drawers, locked.'

Wycliffe looked through the haul: passports for the family, none of the stamps less than three years old; birth certificates, marriage lines; a couple of policies, one for the van; a few bank statements, and an envelope boldly marked with a date: 15·4·79.

Fox said: 'One of the other drawers is stuffed full of letters but I haven't had a chance to go through them yet.'

Wycliffe was intrigued by the dated envelope but all it held was a press cutting:

Professional Men's Annual Dinner
Nearly a hundred members of the West Cornwall Association of Professional Men, with their guests, attended their annual dinner at The Royal Hotel on Easter Saturday. Mr Ernest Bishop, retiring chairman, presided, and the guest speaker was Mr Gerald Bateman MP. The theme of Mr Bateman's address was the need to maintain high standards of integrity and independence in the face of growing domination of the professions by central and local government . . .

And three bags full! Why had Lemarque kept this cutting along with things which he obviously regarded as important?

Wycliffe said: 'I'll take this and give you a receipt.'

He left Fox to his work and crossed the landing to Francine's room. He stood in the small space between bed and chest of drawers, looking about him. Francine's school books were on two shelves above the chest of drawers. In addition to her textbooks there was a pile of exercise books, neatly arranged: Mathematics, English, Chemistry, French, Biology, History . . . Wycliffe flicked through some of them. The handwriting was more sophisticated than he would have expected from a girl of her age; the marks were average, the comments often acid. On the chest itself there was a swing mirror, a sketch pad and a box of watercolours, along with a few cosmetic jars and bottles. He tried the drawers, the top left-hand one, the only one fitted with a lock, was quite empty. The other top drawer held a jumble of underclothes and a box of cheap jewellery – beads, bracelets, rings and earrings. The other drawers were given over to clothes.

The empty drawer was where she had kept those things without which the little room became anonymous. Her letters, cards, snapshots, sketches, and all the other trifles she had thought worth keeping. She had taken them with her – or she had destroyed them.

Jane Lemarque had been murdered and her husband was missing, yet Wycliffe's thoughts still centred on their runaway daughter. He could not rid himself of the memory of the girl in the blue dress who, in that little grey church, had evoked the Madonna; remote, mysterious, and deeply moving in her sad presentiment: ' . . . and purple for Death.' Twenty minutes later she had been picked up by the youth in the red car.

'Francine is a very talented girl but she can be difficult . . . if she thought she had a real grievance . . . Young Paul will have his problems if their friendship ever comes to anything.' Virginia.

'It wouldn't surprise me if she had gone off with some man, and I mean, man.' Caroline.

Then there was the story of Francine and her mother's watch.

The Lizzie Borden fantasy was bizarre but he felt in his bones that the runaway girl held the key to her mother's murder.

He returned his attention to the rest of the room. No desk, no table, not even a chair. Probably she had done her homework sitting up in bed, scribbling away with a ball-point while pop music kept the silence at bay. Her radio was on the floor within reach of her hand. The bed was a divan with a narrow gap underneath to accommodate the castors. He knelt down, felt underneath, and came out with a little paper-covered notebook and a ball-point pen. One up on Curtis! But no real score. Most of the pages had been torn from the notebook and the remaining five or six had been used for notes on biology. There were headings: Eye Colour, Hair Colour, Skin Pigmentation, Blood . . . with brief notes under each and, in one case, a diagram.

Heredity. Wycliffe had only vague notions on the subject, derived from elementary lessons at school on the breeding prospects of peas and little red-eyed flies. He put the notebook back where he had found it.

Curtis was right, the girl had made sure that nobody would learn much from her room. In fact, he could get no feeling anywhere in the house that it had been really lived in, only that people had camped out there.

A voice at the bottom of the stairs said: 'Mr Wycliffe! Mr Kersey is here, sir.'

The return of the prodigal. Warmth on both sides.

'Good to be back, sir! Like old times.' The difference being that Kersey was now an inspector instead of a sergeant. 'The van is parked by the church and D.C. Dixon is duty officer, so we are in business.'

Now they had a base linked in to the police communication network as well as the public telephone service.

The two men had always worked well together though physically and temperamentally they were very different. Wycliffe, spare, thin-featured, thin-lipped, and sandy-haired, nick-named The Monk. Kersey, stocky of build, full of face, very dark, with features which looked as though they had been roughly moulded out of plasticene and carelessly stuck on. By the same token, Wycliffe was taciturn and inclined to be prudish in speech and attitude, while Kersey often thought aloud and was not averse to what he called basic English. Together, they drove back to the village.

At Mynhager the family would be sitting down to their Christmas meal: turkey with all the trimmings, pudding with clotted cream, (cholesterol by the spoon-ful), plenty of wine; crackers to pull, and flushed faces afterwards. In the village people were beginning to take an interest in what was going on. Although it was quite dark people were standing in their doorways, others had the curtains drawn back in their front-rooms. Not that there was much to see.

The van was parked near the wall of the churchyard and opposite the village's two shops, now closed for the holiday. Inside the van the radio crackled in staccato outbursts: 'Alpha one-four to Alpha Victor. I am attending an R.T.A. at . . . ' 'Alpha Victor to Alpha three. A householder at Nance Cottage, Sancreed, reports an intruder in her garden . . . '

A disturbance by youths on motorcycles in a car-park, a Ford Escort saloon apparently abandoned . . . The bread and butter of police work.

D.C. Dixon had a mug of tea at his elbow, already somebody was pecking away at a typewriter in the next cubicle, the van was an old model and had the authentic smell of a nick. The blinds were down and there was an atmosphere of stuffy cosiness; some wag had suspended a sprig of mistletoe from one of the roof struts. Home from home.

Dixon had news: 'Message from D.S. Curtis, sir. He's

on his way here with Timothy Pellowe. He said you
would understand.'

So Pellowe and his red car had, presumably, been
picked up on their doorstep. And Francine?

While they were waiting Wycliffe put Kersey in the
picture.

Timothy Pellowe was lean and lank and pale, a weed
grown in poor soil and a bad light. At nineteen he
retained an adolescent spottiness, and the inability to
cope with his legs and arms. He sprawled over a chair
and on to the small table which separated him from
Wycliffe. They were in the interview cubicle of the van;
Kersey sat by the door, just out of the boy's line of sight.

'I was staying with a friend in Exeter; we had a party
last night and it was lunch time before I was up. Then,
on the news, I heard about Mrs Lemarque. They said
the police wanted to contact her husband and daughter;
then they said the police wanted to interview the driver
of a red Triumph and they gave my number . . . ' His
voice faltered. 'It was as if they thought . . . ' Words
failed him.

'You were asked to go to the nearest police station;
why didn't you?'

The muscles round his right eye twitched in a nervous
tic. 'I was scared; I mean, once the police get hold of you
. . .' He realized that he was not being diplomatic and
dried up.

'So what did you do?'

'I drove home and told father; he said I should talk to
Mr Curtis and explain to him.'

'Now Mr Curtis has brought you here, so you can
explain to me. Where is Francine?'

The pale blue eyes sought Wycliffe's in pathetic
appeal. 'I don't know – honest to God I don't. I—'

'When did you last see her?'

'The night before last when I dropped her off outside
Exeter railway station; she said she was catching a train

and that the lift would save her a good chunk of the fare.'

'What time was it?'

He frowned: 'I picked her up just down the road here at a bit before half-nine, so it must've been about half-eleven when I dropped her.' His manner became petulant, as with a child coming near to tears. 'Like I said, I just gave her a lift . . . I haven't done anything!'

'Obviously you picked her up by arrangment; when was the arrangment made?'

'She rang me up that morning. She knew I was going to Exeter for Christmas and that I was driving up that evening. She asked me to pick her up in the village between a quarter and half after nine. It just meant going a bit later than I intended to; no bother.'

Pellowe turned his uneasy gaze on Kersey who looked about as reassuring as a lion working up an appetite for his next Christian.

Wycliffe persisted: 'Did she say why she wanted the lift – where she was going?'

'She said she was going to spend Christmas with relatives, that was all. Fran never says much, I mean, she never really tells you anything.'

'Did you know that her parents had no idea that she was going away?'

'Of course I didn't! How could I? She said she was going to stay with relatives.'

'How did you meet her?'

'At a disco in St Ives. She goes there most Friday nights and she would let me take her home.' Naive in his humility.

'And after school? You picked her up from school sometimes?'

Pellowe nodded. 'A couple of times.'

Kersey said: 'Did you have it off with her?'

The boy jumped. 'By God! She's not that sort!'

'No? What sort is she, then?'

He hesitated. 'It's hard to say. I mean, I don't think any other girl could get away with it.'

'With what?'

He searched for words. 'Well, you have to make all the running; she never sort of meets you half-way, but she can still take her pick.'

'And she picked you?'

The boy was not stupid; he saw the point. 'Yes, well, I never try anything on, I mean nothing much. I know she won't stand for it.' He grinned for the first time. 'Only last week a bloke got a bit randy with her; she poured a whole glass of iced coke down his jeans and said: "Better if chilled before serving".'

'According to you she doesn't say a lot, but you must have been with her for a couple of hours in the car on your way to Exeter. What did you talk about?'

He shook his head. 'We didn't. When I tried she just said, "Oh, shut up, Timmy! I'm trying to think." Of course it isn't always like that; she can be very sort of friendly and nice.'

More questions, but no more revealing answers. In the end Wycliffe left him with a D.C. to make his statement.

Kersey said: 'A made-to-measure Wet!'

Wycliffe was thoughtful. 'I wonder if she's with her father.'

'It's a possibility.'

The investigation was getting off the ground. Four men, working in pairs, had started house-to-house enquiries. Wycliffe had small hope of picking up any direct leads and the questions were largely camouflage for gossip which he hoped might be a worthwhile harvest.

Sergeant Fox and his team were still at the cottage.

End of a day. Christmas Day.

CHAPTER SIX

Wycliffe opened his eyes and wondered where he was. Light from a street lamp filtered through orange curtains drawn over a small square window. There was a sloping ceiling with beams exposed. Then he remembered: he was staying at The Tributers, and Kersey was in the next room. The rest of the headquarters people were at a boarding house in St Ives. He switched on the bedside lamp to look at his watch: five minutes past seven. Boxing Day. A funny Christmas!

He listened; the silence seemed absolute, then he began to hear the ticking of the grandfather clock at the bottom of the stairs. He felt relaxed. An accommodating landlady had taken them in on Christmas night and fed them on cold turkey with a salad. She had promised them breakfast at eight, earlier than they could reasonably expect over the holiday.

'Think nothing of it, my lovers! If you can find out who 'twas that put a bullet in that poor soul's head then you'll be doing us all a big favour. I can't say I exactly liked the little woman, nor him neither, but I wouldn' wish that on my worst enemy, an' tha's a fact!'

The Tributers had been in the hands of the Tregidgo (second g, soft) family since the early 1800s and Phyllis was first cousin as well as wife to the present owner. 'We've always tried to keep it in close family, sort of,' she said. ''Tis the best way.'

At ten minutes to eight he joined Kersey in the dining-room. Kersey looked like the morning after; dark people are rarely at their best in the morning. 'She asked me if we wanted the full treatment and I said we did.' A delicious smell of frying bacon came from the kitchen next door. 'I don't know about you but I'm not allowed to have it at home; Joan says she wants me to live long enough to draw my pension and that means two rounds of wholemeal toast with margarine scrape, or a bowl of some bloody cereal with bran in it, and black coffee. Sometimes I wonder if it's worth it.'

Phyllis came in with heaped plates: bacon, egg, sausage and tomato. 'Now then! Get that inside of you an' you'll feel better. 'Tis a mucky ol' morning.' Phyllis, at fifty, was plump, clear-skinned and rosy-cheeked, low in polyunsaturates, high in cholesterol.

On the radio, the weather forecast: 'The mild weather over south-west England will continue. Winds will be light and variable and in the extreme south-west mist and fog now affecting coasts and hills will persist for most of the day.'

As the light strengthened they could see that the dining-room looked out on a small patch of garden but the boundary hedge remained insubstantial as a shadow. At intervals the foghorn on Pendeen Watch moaned piteously.

They listened to the eight o'clock News which, in deference to Christmas, tried to mitigate its intrinsic gloom. At the end there was a brief item on the Cornish murder, followed by: 'The police are anxious to contact the husband and daughter of the murdered woman, Alain and Francine Lemarque. Anyone with information which may help to trace them should telephone 0736 212121 or contact their nearest police station.'

At half-past nine, someone did. Wycliffe and Kersey were in the Incident Van. D.C. Potter was duty officer, a man not made to fit into cubicles so that he had difficulty in accommodating himself between desk and partition. He had a bottled gas heater going which made the air steamy instead of merely moist.

In the next cubicle Wycliffe and Kersey heard him take the call.

'Yes, Miss . . . That is correct. Can I have your name, please? . . . No, it isn't essential . . . Yes, I'll put you through to the officer in charge.' Potter being diplomatic for once.

Wycliffe picked up his telephone and switched on the desk amplifier. The girl's voice was harsh and brittle; her manner aggressive. Wycliffe imagined her, thin, angular, mousey-coloured hair, pinched nose, tiny mouth.

'Are you the man in charge?'

'Chief Superintendent Wycliffe.'

'They said on the radio you want to know where Francine Lemarque is. She's at Flat 4, 14, Burbage Street, Camden.'

'Thank you. Is she with her father?'

'I don't know anything about her father; I'm telling you about her. You got the address? 14, Burbage Street, Flat 4.' And she put the phone down.

Potter stood in the doorway. 'That was a pay-phone call, sir.'

Wycliffe said to Kersey. 'More than a bit of spite behind that but it didn't sound like a hoax. We'll check with the Met and get them to make contact. We want her here but if she doesn't want to come it will be difficult; I doubt if we have grounds for compulsion so it will have to be persuasion.'

'She must know about her mother.'

'I shall be surprised if she doesn't but that must be the Met's initial approach, to break the news. Boxing Day: no trains and no coaches. Potter! Find out if there is an afternoon or evening flight from Heathrow to St Mawgan, or even Plymouth. If there is, and the Met can get her on it . . .'

Kersey said, 'We'd better warn them in case her father is with her, we don't want him to slip through our fingers.'

Wycliffe agreed, but casually.

Across the square from the church there were two

shops, and one of them, Mulfra General Stores, was open, a phenomenon unknown in most places on Boxing Day. A constant trickle of customers kept the doorbell jangling. Kersey stood up. 'I want to slip over to the shop.' He had sufficient tact not to mention cigarettes.

Kersey's attempts to kick the habit were regular and only briefly sustained; this was an interregnum but he was resolved to try again in the New Year. Wycliffe watched him cross the square. No doubt the shop also sold pipe tobacco. He sucked the end of his ball-point and reflected that human existence was a long sad story of self-denial. Then he saw Marsden making for the shop, carrying a shopping bag, and ploughing along like an old Thames barge under full sail.

Kersey returned with a question: 'Did you see the chap who came into the shop after me?'

'A big fellow with dark curly hair?'

'Yes.'

'That's Marsden, the painter who found the body. His statement came in this morning. What about him?'

'I've seen him before somewhere.'

'He's not the sort you'd be likely to forget.'

Kersey brooded. 'It was a good while ago and he didn't have the trim on his upper lip, but I'm damned if I can remember when it was or in what connection.'

'You think you've come across him professionally?'

'I'm sure of it.'

'Then you'd better try to remember.'

'It's no good forcing it.' Kersey was thoughtful. 'What's he like, apart from his looks?'

'I think he could cut up rough if provoked. He's fond of women, very much in the plural. For what it's worth I'd say he's a good painter. He plays jazz music very loud . . . Oh, yes, and he's got a cat called Percy.' Kersey looked at his chief, puzzled. Even after years of working together there were still quirks of character which he could never understand. 'They took his prints yesterday for elimination purposes so if you have any suspicion we can check with C.R.O.'

On Wycliffe's table little heaps of typescript had begun to grow and in yet another cubicle a D.C. was going full-hammer to maintain the supply. Wycliffe put on his spectacles. Franks had dictated a memo over the telephone, his preliminary report. No revelations. Jane Lemarque had died of 'injuries to her head and neck inflicted by a heavy calibre bullet which had entered in the region of the axis vertebra and pursued a complex course through the skull to exit anteriorly through the face, destroying a large area around the bridge of the nose, and affecting the eyes and the orbits on both sides. The trajectory suggests that the deceased might have been in a crouching position at the time the shot was fired. This would be consistent with her position when the body was found, between the bed and the dressing table.'

Regarding the time of death, Franks showed his usual caution: 'Death probably occurred at some time between four in the afternoon and eight in the evening of the 24th.'

'The poor woman was cornered and trying to shield herself by squeezing under the bed,' Wycliffe said. 'It looks more and more like cold-blooded murder.'

Kersey agreed. 'But cut out passion and you have to look for a rational motive.'

Wycliffe doodled on a scrap pad. 'We've got to know more about what went on in that house before and after Lemarque came out of jail.'

'The girl should be a help there.'

The girl – Francine, the Virgin in the blue gown. Once more Wycliffe recalled the deep impression she had made on him with her air of total detachment. Marsden, in his painting, had interpreted it as self absorption. Perhaps he was right. Anyway, what did it matter? Irritably, he pushed his doodle aside – a thing of triangles and squares. 'I think that we shall get from the girl only what she chooses to tell us, but I'm hoping for another angle from the chaps on house-to-house. The woman can't have lived in complete isolation while her husband was in jail, there must be someone who can claim to know her.'

Kersey was turning over a slim bundle of question-naires already completed in house-to-house enquiries. 'There's not a lot here. The locals seem generally anti-Lemarque but on no specific grounds. I get the impression that outsiders are simply unwelcome and if you happen to be one you have to keep running to stay where you are.' He flipped through the pages. 'There is something though: Two people say they saw Lemarque's van being driven through the village on Saturday afternoon – Christmas Eve. It was travelling in the direction of Pendeen. One of them says Lemarque was driving.'

'At least that ties up with what Marsden told us.' Wycliffe sounded bored.

Kersey took the hint and stood up. 'I'll get on to the Met and ask them to check that address. We should have something from them during the morning.'

'One more thing: we need to know something about Lemarque. I want H.Q. to go to work on the story of the Lemarque/Bateman partnership. What were they up to? What went wrong? And what precisely landed Lemarque in jail? Anything which helps to put the man in focus.'

'I'll pass the word.'

Left alone, Wycliffe tried to take stock. Of the Lemarque family, Jane Lemarque had been murdered, and her husband and daughter were missing. He now had a line on the girl but none on her father. Passports for all three had been found in a drawer of the dressing table and among a few letters in a sideboard drawer downstairs, there was an address for Jane's sister in Bristol. She was being contacted through her local police. Fox had reported that most of the clothes in the

95

main bedroom wardrobe belonged to Lemarque: three good suits, a couple of raincoats, and an overcoat, as well as a good range of casual clothes; relics of past prosperity. Impossible to say what he might have taken with him, but Fox's guess was, very little. Not, apparently, a planned exit.

Wycliffe was staring out of the window of his cubicle. A few yards away in a bay-window of one of the larger houses, a little old man in a tartan dressing gown was seated in some sort of wheelchair and he seemed to be returning Wycliffe's stare but his old eyes were probably too weak to focus at the distance. Behind him the light caught the shiny balls on a Christmas tree.

The scene-of-crime people had now finished at the cottage; some material had gone to the forensic laboratories for the boffins to brood over, including the fatal bullet and a nine-millimetre cartridge case, but the fingerprint and photographic evidence was at headquarters for processing. No joy yet, and forensic eggs are sometimes addled before they have the chance to hatch.

Which left the house-to-house enquiries, and they had produced little so far. But he had not yet tackled the most promising of the houses.

He could hear Kersey's voice in the next cubicle, talking to somebody at the Met. Time to stir himself. *Courage mon brave!* He said to Potter: 'I shall be at Mynhager.'

He got into his car and drove past the pub along the track to Mynhager and the sea. Mist enveloped the moors and rolled down the slopes, dissolving and condensing by turns, so that the near landscape was at one moment clearly seen and at the next, entirely hidden. He felt blinkered, and lowered the car window in the hope of better vision. Although there was no breath of wind a sea swell, aftermath of the storm, continued to break along the shore with a booming sound which reverberated up the valley, through the fog.

He parked in the courtyard of Mynhager and went round the house to the front door. The terrace was drenched in spray from the last tide. Caroline answered his ring.

She seemed surprised and pleased to see him. 'Charles!' She looked behind her into the hall and lowered her voice. 'Come in.' Her manner was almost conspiratorial. 'In here! Ernest has gone out.' She led him into Ernest's little office and closed the door. 'I wanted to talk to you, Charles, but I didn't want to be seen going to your caravan thing by the church. Do sit down.'

Caroline in slacks and a woolly jumper. A different and diffident Caroline, uneasy, perhaps in search of reassurance. She looked pale, her eyes were puffy with tiredness and she had been drinking. 'I'm worried, Charles. I suppose I can talk to you? I mean, if what I tell you isn't directly relevant to . . . to Jane's death, it won't go any further, will it?'

'If it really isn't relevant, no.'

She was sitting in Ernest's swivel chair, swinging from side to side like a nervous child. 'Hugh Marsden was taken to the police station to make a statement, because he found her. At least I suppose that was the reason. You see, I can't find out anything; I mean, Hugh isn't on the phone, and as things are I daren't go there . . . ' She paused, apparently in the hope of getting some encouragement, but Wycliffe merely looked at her, benevolently non-committal, and she went on: 'You must have guessed if you haven't already been told, that Gerald and I are not the ideal married couple. We keep going for Paul's sake and for appearances generally.' Another pause, then: 'He's my cousin, you know – mother's twin sister's child. He used to spend a lot of time here when mother was alive. I don't know why I married him – he was handy, I suppose.'

'Why are you telling me this?'

She wriggled in her chair, easing her slacks round her

97

thighs like a man. 'Because I've been having an affair with Marsden off and on for the past two years.'

'So?'

'My God! You don't make it easy! I'm trying to tell you that I know Hugh Marsden very well; he confides in me; we are good friends, quite apart from the other thing.' She was staring out of the window though there was nothing to see but the grubby net curtain and the mist beyond. 'There are no strings; I don't care a damn about his reputation.'

'You mean that your relationship with him is different – special.'

She turned on him angrily then decided against aggression. 'All right, damn you! – yes. As a matter of fact he's getting rid of the girl who lives with him; she's never been much more than a housekeeper anyway.'

Wycliffe wondered where all this was leading but he asked no questions.

She came out with it abruptly: 'Is Hugh under suspicion?'

'He wasn't detained after making his statement.'

She made a derogatory gesture. 'That's a big help!' She hesitated, then went on: 'Of course I know he's had other women, everybody knows it; what they don't know is that one of those women was Jane Lemarque – just the once, while Alain was in jail.'

'So?'

A look of intense exasperation. 'Jane, being the fool she is – was, might have told Alain when he came out.'

Wycliffe was beginning to see light through the fog. 'Presumably Marsden told you.'

'Only because I made him tell me about his other women.'

'Are you suggesting that the incident between Jane Lemarque and Marsden gave her husband a motive for murdering her?'

She looked at him quickly and away again. 'I don't know about that. I've told you this because I'm pretty sure Hugh won't. You mightn't think so but he has scruples about things and they could land him in trouble.'

'I see. You think that when we find Lemarque all this could come out anyway.'

No answer. He imagined that as far as Caroline was concerned their *tête à tête* was now over but she had more to say: 'There's something else. I shouldn't have said what I did about Francine yesterday. About her going off with a man and the idea that she might . . . Well, what Aunt Stella said was obvious nonsense and I shouldn't have encouraged her.'

'You've seen her portrait?'

She had been staring out of the window and she turned on him, ready to spit fire, but once more she changed her mind and managed a sheepish grin instead. 'You're a clever bastard in some ways. I suppose when it comes down to it I'm like any other woman where a man is concerned, I can cope with competition from my own age group but if it comes to teenagers . . . '

Wycliffe said: 'In this case I don't think it has.'

She looked at him, surprised. 'No? Well, thanks for that anyway.' She got up. 'I suppose you came to see Ernest but, as I told you, he's out. He should be back in time for lunch.'

Wycliffe remained seated. 'I came to talk to your husband.'

She seemed surprised. 'Gerald? Gerald has gone to lunch with one of his party cronies in Penzance. God knows when he'll be back. Late this afternoon, probably.'

'Is Paul about?'

'Paul? He's gone out walking with his uncle.' She saw Wycliffe glance out of the window at the fog. 'I know; they're both mad.'

'Perhaps you will tell Paul that we have some news of Francine. An anonymous telephone caller said that she was staying at an address in Camden. That was all; but we are arranging for someone to go to that address and, if she is there, they will try to persuade her to come home.'

A mocking grin; something of the old Caroline. 'My, my! There is, after all, someone in this house who's managed to kindle a spark. Anyway, I'll tell him!'

Wycliffe got up to go. 'Just two more questions: How long has Marsden lived down here?'

'About four years, perhaps a bit more.'

'Have you any idea where he came from?'

'Why don't you ask him?' Aggressive.

'Perhaps I will. I wonder if I am allowed to ask if he rents or owns the cottage?'

She relented. 'Sorry! People have it in for Hugh just because he doesn't fit into any of their mean little pigeon holes. Before he came here he lived in London – Bayswater, I think. The cottage belongs to us. Believe it or not there is a Bishop Estates Limited in which we all have shares. It's some sort of tax wangle, I think. When my great-great-grandfather built the place he bought the whole valley and the farms on both sides.'

'Thank you.'

'You said there were two questions.'

'So I did! I wonder if you remember whether the Lemarques were down here for Easter '79?'

She frowned. 'I can't remember '79 especially but they never missed being here for Easter. Why?'

'Just routine.'

Poor Caroline! A real home-loving Cornish girl but unable to do without sex and preferably sex without a husband cluttering up the place.

As she was seeing him off in the hall, Joseph came down the stairs. 'Wycliffe!' The old man descended the remaining three or four steps. 'No news of Lemarque?'

'Not so far.'

'And Francine?'

'It seems she's staying at a flat in Camden; we've had an anonymous call and we're following it up.'

Joseph laughed. 'She'll give you a run for your

money, that one! She's one of the new breed, Wycliffe. The future, if there is one, belongs to the women. Do you realize that? They're flexing their muscles, testing their strength; come the sexual revolution, Francine and her kind will be the brains behind it. Have you heard the latest R.C. joke? At the next Vatican conference bishops will bring their wives. At the one after that the Pope will bring her husband. Thank God I shall be dead by then! Anyway, don't let me detain you; I'm off for my walk.'

'Not in this fog, father!'

Joseph looked at his daughter. 'Your time is not yet, my child. A man can still make some decisions for himself.'

CHAPTER SEVEN

Without much conviction Wycliffe supposed that he must be making progress. Seemingly unrelated events were falling into an intelligible pattern and what more could he ask? Lemarque, having been home for a matter of weeks, learns from his wife that she has been to bed with the painter. Surely more than enough to raise the tension in the Lemarque household. Francine, caught in the middle, decides to get out, presumably until the worst is over. Then, on Christmas Eve night, with matters made worse by Francine running away, Lemarque, in a blazing row, loses all control and shoots his wife. Exit Lemarque.

Tidy. Tidy and simple. Most homicides turn out that way when you are lucky enough to pick up the right lead. Now they were on the track of the girl and the next step was to find Lemarque and charge him.

In his mind's eye Wycliffe saw the little man: the solemn features of a clown, the long-limbed, agile frame of a monkey. He recalled Lemarque sitting in the dismal living-room of the cottage, trying to play second fiddle to his wife who refused to play at all. A killer? Well, there must be a great deal more to him than appeared that morning. He had helped to build a very successful business and he had shown sufficient resolution to stay with it against the odds. Foolish, perhaps, but neither stupid nor weak.

He parked his car by the police van and went in. The clock over Potter's table showed twenty minutes to twelve. The lights were on in the van, fighting the gloom of the morning.

Potter said: 'A nice mug of coffee? Keep the fog out.'

But Wycliffe was irritable. 'You missed your calling, Potter: a white coat and a coffee bar in Cornwall Street. Is Mr Kersey in?'

'Next door, sir.'

Kersey was waiting for him. 'The Met really got their skates on. I had their report a few minutes ago. The Burbage Street flat is occupied by three girls and a boy, students at the Poly. Oh, to be eighteen again! In my day you had to make do with the shop doorway furthest from the street lamp. But I'll bet they've got that poor stupe doing the cooking and the washing-up. Anyway, two of the girls went home to mummy for the Christmas hols, leaving a cosy *ménage à deux* until Francine turned up. Unexpected, according to Cuthbert. Believe it or not, that's his name. It seems she had a school-kid thing going with him when they both lived in Richmond, ring-a-roses in the park, and they've kept in touch. He's a couple of years older, of course, and is a bit coy about it now. One gathers his flatmate wasn't enthusiastic about Francine's arrival but they let her stay.'

'How did she explain, turning up there like that?'

'The universal password: getting away from the family.'

'At some stage they must have heard about the shooting.'

'Not until this morning. It seems that the young miss who phoned us got up early. That means any time up to eleven, and she heard our bit on the radio. Instead of telling the others she went out to a public box and phoned us. When she got back she woke her boyfriend and they decided to confront Francine.'

'Well?'

'They couldn't. The bird had flown.'

'When?'

'They reckon she must have gone during the night or early morning. She had a radio in her room and she probably heard the news before they did.'

'So we are back to square one.'

'Except that we know she isn't with papa.'

'Wasn't with papa, you mean.' Wycliffe was not pleased; he had counted on making contact with the girl, even if it had to be at second-hand.

Kersey said: 'She may be trying to get home but with no public transport she's likely to have problems.'

'Anything else?'

'The Bristol aunt telephoned – Jane Lemarque's sister, a Mrs Devlin; she's on her way down by car. Sounds prosperous and capable.'

'I'm glad somebody is.'

Kersey said: 'It's still Christmas. What about a drink before lunch? Phyllis told me she serves a genuine home-brew in the bar. They get it from a brother in Helston or some place.'

'Nobody cares a damn! It's Christmas. No newspapers, no trains, no buses, no mail; the television squeezing out strawberry mousse with whipped cream topping. This week has been cancelled; the whole country is in a coma.'

Kersey grinned, mellowed by the Tregidgo home-brew: 'Scrooge!'

But Wycliffe was not to be diverted. 'At any other time Lemarque's van would have been spotted and we should be getting reports of him having been seen anywhere and everywhere between the Isle of Mull and Oxford Street.'

'Don't tell me you miss our friends of the press?'

'Perverted as it may be, I do.'

It was half-past two, they were back in the Incident Van; Dixon had replaced Potter on the desk. There was a tap at the door and D.C. Curnow came in, one of the house-to-house team. A young giant, he had to stoop to clear the lintel.

'I've just come from 6, Wesley Terrace, sir, a Mrs Evadne Penrose, a widow. She says she was a close friend of the dead woman and that they were in touch on Christmas Eve, the day of the murder.'

'And she's just remembered it?'

'No, sir. She spent Christmas with her mother in Padstow and didn't hear about the murder until she got back this morning.'

'Well?'

'She won't talk to me; it has to be "the officer in charge" and she won't come here, though God knows why not.'

'What's she like?'

An amused grin. 'Very forthright and she talks a lot about astrology.'

'Kinky?'

'I wouldn't say kinky, sir, eccentric.' D.C. Curnow had a nice feeling for words. 'I think she's probably reliable.'

Wesley Terrace was a row of sizeable cottages near the Mechanics' Institute and number six was double-fronted. The front door was provided with a cast-iron knocker in the shape of a lion's head. Wycliffe knocked and the door was answered by a small, thin woman with sharp features and frizzy, greying hair cut short.

'Mrs Penrose?'

'Evadne Penrose. You must be the chief superintendent.' Almost an accusation.

Wycliffe was shown into an over-furnished little room which reminded him of the parlour of the farmhouse in which he had been born. There was a three-piece suite, an upright piano, a chiffonier, a fireplace with brass fire-irons, and framed coloured prints on the walls.

'I'm sorry to get you here but when I have something to say I believe in saying it to the man in charge but I didn't fancy going along to that hut on wheels in the square.' Her brown eyes darted fierce glances, like a firecracker giving off sparks, and her bony little paw gripped like a pincers. 'Do sit down.'

'You knew Mrs Lemarque?'

A vigorous nod. 'I was Jane's friend, perhaps her only

105

friend. After that terrible business with Alain going to prison I could see that she needed someone. Apart from anything else there was the dramatic change in their circumstances. She lost everything! Of course, the people round here are terribly clannish; they've no room for outsiders, and they tolerate me only because my husband was one of them ... You don't mind if I smoke?' She brought out a cigarette pack from the pocket of her woollen frock, lit one and inhaled like a deprived addict.

Wycliffe made a bid for the initiative. 'We need to know more about Mrs Lemarque, about the family and their connections. As a friend, you may be able to help if you are ready to be quite frank.'

She had perched herself on the arm of the settee. 'But that's why I've asked you to come here, so that I can be frank! That's why I'm talking to you instead of to your young men who are making the rounds like Kleeneeze salesmen.'

Wycliffe tried again. 'You became friendly with Jane Lemarque after her husband went to prison?'

'I knew her long before that; they were down here quite a lot, either staying with the Bishops or at their cottage, but it was only after the calamity that I really got to know Jane. I made a point of it, because I could see that she was a woman at the end of her tether, and when I see something that needs doing, I do it.' A pause for this to sink in. 'I'm a Sagittarian, you know. Poor Jane was a Piscean; emotionally dependent, incapable of any decisive action. I spotted her at once, I wonder if you've noticed that Pisceans can sometimes be recognized by their slightly protruding eyes and vacant expressions?

'No wonder there was stress in their marriage. Alain is an Arien.' Evadne looked around for an ashtray.

Wycliffe said: 'So the Lemarque marriage was not a success?'

Evadne snorted irritably. 'My dear man! I've just told you it was a disaster! They were incompatibles. Alain is

106

vigorous, aggressive, demanding, while Jane was merely passive. I can assure you that Ariens expect more from a woman than passivity; I was married to one. Aries is the sign of the Ram.'

Wycliffe felt a pang of sorrow for the late Mr Penrose who, Arien or not, must have lived out his married life under a constant threat of being eaten.

'I understand that Lemarque was fond of his wife.'

'In the same way as you might be fond of a cat. All is well as long as the cat purrs, rubs round your legs, and jumps on to your lap. Alain's fondness demanded continuous recognition, a constant response, but Pisceans are incapable of any sort of constancy or, indeed, of any deep emotion. And when they find themselves in double harness with an Arien . . . ' She left the prospect to his imagination.

'The point is that after Alain came out of prison they found it even more difficult to live together.' She lowered her voice. 'Neither of them was the sort to clear the air with a row, so they each suffered in their own way and in silence.' Through the haze of tobacco smoke she fixed Wycliffe with an unblinking stare, and spoke slowly, emphasizing her words: 'Jane was afraid that Alain would commit suicide. I told her there was no risk of that with an Arien but she was convinced that she had let him down so badly that he would kill himself. Apparently he had a gun.'

'He had a gun?' Wycliffe did his best not to seem unduly interested.

'So she said; it seems he got it when they were living in Richmond and had all sorts of valuable antiques and pictures in the house.'

'You were in touch with Jane on the day she died?'

'Indeed I was. She telephoned; she often did when she was depressed and alone.'

'At what time did you speak to her?'

'At half-past four.'

'You are sure of that?'

'Quite sure. I was on the point of leaving to spend Christmas with my mother and sister when the phone rang. I said to myself: "Half-past four! I'm late already!" Of course it was Jane. The usual thing: she was depressed and she was sure that Alain was going to kill himself and that if he did it would be her fault. She said that he had gone out soon after lunch and that she was alone when the policeman came about Francine. She'd just been to the drawer of the dressing table where he kept his gun, the drawer was locked but she found a key that fitted, and there was no gun there; it had gone.' Evadne sighed. 'I didn't think Alain was likely to kill himself so I didn't take it very seriously. Of course, I wish I had now. But I did ask her how long it was since she had last seen the gun and she couldn't remember. When it came to the point, she wasn't even sure if she'd seen it since they left Richmond.'

For the first time she looked at Wycliffe with a certain diffidence. 'I suppose he shot her? I don't think that possibility had ever occurred to her, or me . . .'

Wycliffe went off at a tangent: 'I suppose it was the strain between her parents that induced Francine to go away?'

'Of course! Why else would she walk out like that? I admit that she's a difficult girl and sometimes I've felt like giving her a good slap but she's had a hard time in many ways and, of course, she's a Scorpio. You know what that means.'

Wycliffe didn't and didn't want to. He got up from his chair. 'You've been very helpful, Mrs Penrose. I'll send someone along to take your formal statement.'

She came with him to the door and watched while he walked along the street towards the van.

Kersey said: 'Any joy, sir?'

'Lemarque had a gun, at least he had when he was living in Richmond, and Jane Lemarque was speaking to our widow on the telephone at four-thirty on Christmas Eve afternoon.'

108

'Is the woman sure?'

'There is nothing of which Evadne Penrose is not sure including, as far as I could tell, that Lemarque shot his wife because she didn't purr when she was stroked. But to be fair, I think she's probably reliable in matters of fact.'

A girl's voice in the next cubicle, talking to Dixon. A tap on the door and Dixon came in. 'Francine Lemarque, sir.'

She stood in the doorway. She wore jeans and an anorak, both darkened by rain and obviously soaked through. Her dripping hair hung round her shoulders in rat's tails and her face was wet. She looked pale and very tired.

For a long moment Wycliffe just stared at her; he found it hard to accept that this was the girl he had last seen as the Virgin in the blue gown.

'Are you the man in charge?'

'Chief Superintendent Wycliffe.' Absurdly, he felt uncomfortable under the girl's steady gaze.

'I remember you were staying with the Bishops.' She spoke as though recalling something which had happened a long time ago.

Wycliffe, recovering his poise, said: 'How did you get here? You were in London last night.'

'I hitched. I was lucky; I did it in two hops as far as Truro. Last night I heard on the radio what had happened to my mother. They said on the radio that she was shot; is that true?'

'I'm afraid so.'

'And you think he did it?'

'We don't know who did it; we are trying to find out. Naturally we want to speak to your father but so far we haven't been able to find him.'

He was puzzled by her manner; she was certainly distressed, but her strongest emotion was incredulity. 'Don't you think you should get into some dry clothes? We can talk afterwards.'

109

She ignored him. 'Whoever did it must have had a gun.'

'Some time ago your mother told Mrs Penrose that your father had a gun which he got when you lived in Richmond.'

A momentary hesitation. 'Yes he did, a revolver. I remember him showing me how it worked and explaining how dangerous it was. He was always afraid of being burgled in those days. Are you saying that my mother was shot with that gun?'

'You said it was a revolver?'

'Yes, it had a cylinder thing where you put the bullets. I asked you if you thought my mother was shot with that gun?'

'She wasn't shot with a revolver.'

'Well, then!'

Wycliffe saw trouble ahead. In the Children and Young Persons' Act, 1969, a child is defined as someone under the age of fourteen; a young person is someone over the age of fourteen but under eighteen. So here was a young person. He was vague about the provisions of the Act affecting young persons in need of care but his heart sank at the thought of becoming the meat in the sandwich between Francine and some dragon of a social worker. Then he remembered and thanked God for the Bristol aunt.

'Your aunt is on her way down from Bristol; she should be here shortly.'

'Aunt Alice. I hardly know her.'

'When she comes we can make some arrangements: where you will stay and who will look after you. At the moment we don't know where your father is.'

'Why can't I stay at the house and look after myself?'

'That isn't possible, certainly not while the police investigation lasts.'

He had not said one word of sympathy nor offered any consolation. He felt as though he had been justifying himself. Absurd!

110

She stood for a moment as though making up her mind then she said: 'All right! But if I can't stay at the house I need to collect some things from my room.'

'I'll take you down there.'

He picked up her holdall and took her out to the car. She got in, fastened her seat belt and sat there perfectly composed.

The old mine track to the cottage was even more rutted and pot-holed than the one to Mynhager and the mists were going to outlive the day. It must have been a desperately sad and depressing homecoming, but she gave no sign.

'Have you had anything to eat?'

'I had a snack in Truro.'

'This must have been a very great shock to you.'

'Yes.'

He could think of nothing more to say.

He parked the car and they climbed the steps to the front door. He fumbled with the key in the lock and she said: 'Give it to me; there's a knack.' Then, inside: 'I want to collect a few things from my room.'

He almost told her to go ahead but thought better of it. He did not want her in her parents' room. 'I'll come up with you.'

He followed her up the stairs on to the landing. 'Why don't you go into the bathroom and dry yourself?'

'Where shall I be staying?'

'At The Tributers I suppose, until your aunt comes at least.'

She went into the bathroom, taking her bag with her, and ten minutes later, came out with her hair in a frizzy mass, wearing a dry pair of jeans and a woolly top. She spent some time in front of the little swing mirror in her bedroom, brushing her hair until it looked like a TV shampoo advertisement.

Although Wycliffe was watching her from the landing, she behaved exactly as though he wasn't there and he began to wonder why he was. It had been one of those spot decisions which, if they turn out to be justified, are credited to a good copper's instinct.

She was going through her drawers, putting selected items into a travelling case which she brought from the landing cupboard. Finally she snapped the catches shut and straightened up. 'All right.'

He was on the landing and she was in the doorway with her hand on the electric light switch when she suddenly darted back into her room, stooped by the bed, and picked up the little red notebook he had found there. She looked at him with a hint of uncertainty in her manner.

'I might need this; something to write on.'

It was not; for the few pages which remained had already been used. Her uncertainty and the need she had felt to explain were so out of character that he reacted: 'Let me have it, please.'

She held out the little book without hesitation, he took it and slipped it into his pocket. 'You won't mind if I hold on to it for a day or two?'

She looked at him briefly, then turned away.

Alice Devlin was a year or two older than her sister but more animated, more responsive, and Wycliffe liked her on sight. Fortune had dealt with her more kindly. A sporty Sierra, current year; a suede coat, and underneath, a simple frock of some luscious Liberty fabric, definitely not by D.I.Y. out of Pattern Book.

'I knew nothing about it until the police came, I suppose we hadn't been listening to the news over Christmas. It was a shock.' She was clearly upset, grieved, but by no means prostrated. 'Jane and I had gone our separate ways but we had kept loosely in touch; you know the sort of thing: birthday and Christmas cards with the occasional note.'

Her attitude to Francine was warm and sympathetic without being cloying or intrusive. 'You're living through a nightmare, my dear, but it will pass. Try to

112

feel that you are not alone. I don't want to press you but you can come back with me and stay until things are sorted out – or as long as you want. Philip and I would like that.'

They took rooms at The Tributers and Phyllis laid on an early meal. Wycliffe sat in on the meal without taking part and through it all Francine remained quietly aloof. Had she been persuaded out of her eternal jeans? At any rate she wore her woolly jumper with a tartan skirt. Her hair, dry now and shining in the light, was caught back with a clasp. She still looked very tired; her eyes dark, her face pale, her features a trifle pinched. When their meal was over Wycliffe said, 'Now we have to talk.'

Francine's response was immediate; she turned to her aunt. 'I want to talk to him alone.'

'Of course! That's natural.' Understanding woman.

In the Incident Van Wycliffe said: 'Before we start, why don't you ring Paul?'

'Paul? What for?'

'He's been worried about you.'

She hesitated, then: 'All right, if you like.'

Wycliffe said to Dixon: 'Get Paul Bateman on the telephone for me, please.'

When the boy was on the line Wycliffe handed over to Francine.

'Is that Paul? . . . It's me – Francine . . . ' He could hear the boy's elated response but Francine remained casually matter-of-fact. ' . . . No, I'm with the police in their van thing . . . Yes, in the village . . . No, I shouldn't think so . . . I'm all right. My aunt is down . . . I can't talk any more now.' And she put down the telephone.

She and Wycliffe faced each other across the table in the little interview cubicle. Kersey sat by the door. It would have been politic to have a W.P.C. sitting in on the interview but the girl had committed no offence; on the contrary.

'You ran away – why?' Wycliffe's manner was sympathetic, not accusing.

'I didn't run away, I left home.'

'For good?'

'That depended.'

'On what?'

'On whether I could get a job and on what happened at home.'

'Getting a job was bound to take time; how did you intend to live meanwhile?'

'I had money. I've been working in the holidays and saving for a long time.'

'With the idea of leaving home?'

'Perhaps.'

'Why did you make up your mind to go?'

She smoothed her hair away from her eyes with a slow movement of her hand but said nothing.

'Weren't you happy at home?'

'Happy? No, I wasn't.'

'Were your parents unkind to you?'

'No.' She sounded mildly impatient. 'I can't explain; you wouldn't understand. It was like being smothered in cotton wool.'

'Over protective?'

'I told you you wouldn't understand.'

'And things got worse when your father came home?'

'Yes.'

'You blame your mother?'

'I don't blame anybody; mother had to make herself suffer.'

'I don't understand.'

'There's no reason why you should!' With tired indifference.

'As a policeman, I'm afraid there is. Why was the situation worse when your father came home?'

The atmosphere in the little cubicle was claustrophobic. An electric lamp in the low ceiling gave a yellow light which shone on the girl's hair and was reflected dimly off the scuffed and worn plastic surfaces of the walls and fittings. Outside it was quite dark and a blind was drawn over the tiny window. The three of them seemed as isolated as if they had been in a space capsule; the only sound came from sporadic chatter on the radio in the adjoining cubicle.

Kersey said: 'You don't seem to realize, Francine, that we are trying to find out who killed your mother and why.'

She turned to face Kersey then back to Wycliffe. 'When there was just the two of us mother was always explaining how she had failed as a wife or failed me. If it wasn't that, it was how everyone despised her for being such a failure.' She had been looking down at the table top, now she raised her eyes to meet Wycliffe's. 'I think she really believed what she said but she didn't do anything about it. It was so hopeless!' Her voice softened and he thought that she might weep but the moment passed. 'And that Penrose woman with her nonsense about the stars didn't help. "My dear Jane, you are a Piscean! You can't change that!"' For an instant the indomitable Evadne was in the room with them.

Wycliffe persisted: 'But how did your father coming home make things worse?'

'Does it matter?'

'I think you should tell us.'

With a small helpless gesture, still with her eyes on Wycliffe, she said: 'While he was in prison mother let the painter come to the cottage.'

'What do you mean, she let him come to the cottage?'

'All right! She let him go to bed with her.'

'More than once?'

'Not as far as I know.' Indifferent.

'And your father found out?'

'She told him.'

'What happened?'

'Nothing happened.'

'Didn't your father become angry?'

'He was never angry, and that made mother worse. She wanted to be punished.'

Not a trace of emotion; she spoke of her mother, her father, and even of herself, as though none of them had any more significance than the characters in a novel. Once more Wycliffe was aware of the stillness which seemed to envelop this girl like an aura; never once did she fidget, and all her movements were deliberate and controlled. He reminded himself that she was just sixteen, a schoolgirl; he had seen her room with its posters of pop stars, and her school books; in six months time she should be taking her O-levels. She had lost her mother, and her father was missing in suspicious circumstances, yet she fended off any attempt at sympathy or understanding as a boxer parries a blow.

'Did you know about your mother and Marsden when you sat for your portrait with him?'

'She told me.' After a pause: 'Mother had to tell everything. When she couldn't get me to listen she would go and confess to the vicar.'

'The Marsden business didn't upset you?'

She looked at him blankly. 'What difference did it make?'

Was she truly indifferent? Or was she maintaining a profound reserve, refusing to allow him any insight into her mind or her emotions?

He tried another approach. 'You must have planned to go away at least a day or two before you left. Why didn't you leave a note?'

'I did.'

'Both your father and your mother said there was no note.'

'Perhaps they didn't want you to see what was in it.'

'Did you say in the note where you were going?'

'No.'

'What did you say? The kind of things you've told me now?'

'More or less.'

'Have you any idea where your father might be? With a relative, or a friend?'

116

'I've no idea.'

'Who do you think killed your mother?' Gently.

'I don't know. I've sometimes thought that she might take her own life; are you sure that she didn't?'

Wycliffe changed the subject. 'Your father had some idea of going back into business; do you know anything about that?'

'I've heard them talking; something about a tourist park on some waste ground where there used to be mine workings. He was expecting somebody to put up money for it.'

'Did your parents have many outside contacts? I mean, did people visit them, ring them up, or did they go out a lot?'

She shook her head. 'Only the Penrose woman came to our house and sometimes mother would ring her up.'

'And your father?'

'Nobody came to see him but he went out a lot with the van.'

'Did he get phone calls?'

'I think he made his phone calls when I wasn't there.'

'What makes you think so?'

'Because sometimes when I came in he would be on the phone to someone and he would ring off as soon as he could.'

'You realize that anything you can tell us may help to solve the mystery of your mother's death and your father's disappearance. Is there anything you can tell us that you overheard on the phone?'

'No, I didn't take much notice.'

'Did you gather what his phone conversations were about?'

'Oh, about money and business.'

'Were they friendly conversations?'

'Just ordinary. One day last week he seemed to be annoyed. He was almost shouting until he saw me.'

'What was he saying?'

She frowned. 'It didn't make much sense. Something

117

like: "Five years ago we were all in the same boat – or perhaps I should say the same car. Not any more! I no longer belong to the club." Then he turned round and saw me and I realized that I had put him off.'

What more could he ask? He walked back with her to The Tributers. The misty rain had stopped and the weather seemed to be clearing; stars twinkled through rifts in the clouds.

'Good night, Francine.'

'Good night.' Casual.

He was moved by her isolation. Rarely in the thousands of interviews he had conducted had he learned so little of the personality of the other party. Businessmen, lawyers, even the Mr Bigs of the crime world, all gave something of themselves away, but not this girl of sixteen. Although she had answered his questions, at no time had he been allowed a glimpse of her private world; he still had no idea of what she thought or felt, no clue to suggest what she might do. Talking to her was like playing chess with a computer, yet everything about her pointed to an intense emotional life behind the façade.

Kersey said: 'It adds up to Alain Lemarque. When a man murders his wife we look for the instant of passion but Lemarque wasn't that kind of man. The girl says he never got angry; what she means is he didn't show it. In other words, he's the type who's capable of nursing a sense of outrage, coming to a decision and carrying it out. Now we know he had a gun.'

'A revolver according to Francine.'

'Surely she was mistaken!'

'From her description, that seems unlikely. What did you make of her?'

Kersey, although he looked like Red Riding Hood's surrogate grandmother, had two lovely daughters and could be considered something of an authority. 'My guess would be that she's putting up a smoke screen, but why?'

Wycliffe had no answer for that. 'According to Evadne Penrose, Jane Lemarque thought her husband intended to kill himself and Francine seemed to believe that her mother might commit suicide. A suicide pact isn't out of the question, I suppose, though there's every sign that the woman was trying to escape being shot. We just don't know what's happened to Lemarque, whether he's alive or dead.'

They were having their evening meal, waited on by a village girl called Lorna; dark, freckled, and pretty. In the bar next door things were warming up, with the occasional shout and outbursts of laughter, punctuating the general level of chatter. They had spoken quietly with an eye on Lorna's comings and goings but she must have heard something. 'I saw Mr Lemarque's van out to Mennear Bal Saturday afternoon.'

Kersey said: 'That was Christmas Eve.'

'Right first time.'

'The day his wife was shot. You haven't said anything about this before; why not?'

'Well, I wasn't asked, was I? They came and talked to mum and dad but nobody said a word to me. In any case, as I heard it, she was shot in the evening in her own home, and this was in the afternoon between three and four.'

'Where is Mennear Bal?'

'Just a bit down the coast; it's where there used to be mine workings; now 'tis no more 'n a lot of old ruins and heaps of spoil. There's plenty of tracks though and his old van was going slow along the one out near the cliff. My Aunt Flo lives near the workings and she says she seen him down there once before since he was let out of prison. There's a rumour that he's after renting the ground from the mine company though like my dad says, God knows what he thinks he'll do with it.'

'Did you see Lemarque?'

'I didn't see anybody, just the van; I was a good way off. I recognized it because it's the only one around like that.'

119

'And this was definitely at three o'clock?'

She pouted. 'I can't say to the minute but I was home by half-past so it must have been close. I had to walk home and when I got there mother was just leaving to catch the half-past three bus.'

When they were dawdling over their coffee, Wycliffe said: 'It ties up nicely; Marsden saw Lemarque's van being driven towards the village at about three or a bit earlier; it was seen passing through the village in the direction of Pendeen; now we have it among the mine dumps where, apparently, he hoped to build his tourist park. Curtis arrived at the cottage at about 2.45 and Lemarque had already gone. It ties up, without meaning a damn thing as far as we are concerned because, like the girl said, Jane Lemarque wasn't shot at Mennear Bal but in her own home, at some time between four and eight.'

'It looks as though he drove home, shot his wife, then took off.'

Wycliffe was thoughtful. 'Perhaps I saw him leaving.' He told Kersey what he had seen on his way back to Mynhager from the painter's cottage. 'But I don't believe it.'

Lorna came back into the dining-room: 'You're wanted on the telephone.'

He took the call, standing in the passage between the cloakroom and the bar. It was Helen, calling from Kenya.

'I rang Mynhager and spoke to Ernest. He told me you were on a case and gave me another number . . . '

He explained, but contending with the racket from the bar probably meant that his explanation lacked lucidity.

'Anyway, there's nothing wrong with you?' Helen getting down to the things that mattered.

'No, I'm fine. And you?'

'It's nearly midnight here and we've been sitting out

of doors with iced drinks; me in a sleeveless dress. Wish you were here . . . '

'Me too.'

'If I bring home all I've bought, our place is going to look like the Museum of Mankind . . . Well dear, I mustn't run up their bill. Dave and Elsa send their love. Look after yourself, darling. Night . . . '

'I will; and you . . . Night.'

It took him a minute or two to bring himself back.

CHAPTER EIGHT

Jane Lemarque was shot 'with a nine-millimetre automatic, using a parabellum cartridge with a Neonite
propellant. The markings on the bullet and the cartridge case strongly suggest that it was fired from a
Walther P-38.' A dribble of technical jargon from the
ballistics expert. Useful, if they had found a gun or the
person who had used one. There was also a sheaf of
scene-of-crime photographs with a report from Fox,
necessary documentation when and if it came to preparing a case; not much use now. He had reported on
prints found at the cottage: family only, except for
Marsden's prints on the telephone and those of 'one of
the investigating officers'. Fox had tact as well as zeal.

But it hardly looked as though the boffins would
make a great contribution to the case.

Wycliffe and Kersey were in the Incident Van and the
village had a different, more cheerful aspect this
morning, a fine morning after yesterday's gloom: blue
skies, sunshine, and not a breath of wind. An interlude
between fronts, the weathermen said. Both the village
shops were open today and the second one turned out
to be a butcher's.

Already, a green bus had lumbered into the square,
lingered for a minute or two, then moved off without
picking up a single passenger. But, like Noah's olive
leaf, it was a token from an awakening world outside.
Kersey collected a selection of newspapers but the
Cornish murder rated only a few lines on an inside page
of one of them.

The Chief Constable telephoned: Bertram Oldroyd,

a good policeman and a sensitive man, keenly aware of the need to strike a balance between protection and repression. He had a horror of political manipulation. As he grew older in the professional tooth he devoted more of his time to public relations and left the general administration of the force to his departmental heads. He fended off interfering politicians and reserved his most scathing rebukes for those of his staff who lost their footing on the tightrope between Left and Right, Black and White, Pro and Anti.

'Nasty business, Charles! A domestic, I gather.'

'Probably.'

'The girl is safe and sound so that's something. I believe this chap Lemarque was in partnership with Bateman at one time. Any complications from that direction?'

'He seems content to be a spectator at the moment.'

'Good! But you'll need to watch him; he can be a pest.'

'I thought he was on our side.' Wycliffe being naughty.

But Oldroyd only laughed. 'Well, you know what they say: Who needs enemies while we've got friends like him? What about the media?'

'Sleeping off Christmas.'

'Let's hope it stays that way. Heard from Helen?'

'She telephoned last night. David and Elsa are doing her proud.'

'We had a card from her a couple of days before Christmas; give her our love when you're next in touch. But you should be out there, Charles! You take too much on your own shoulders instead of delegating. We're a team – remember?' The big chief chuckled. 'Wasn't it Kant's dove who thought he might fly better in a vacuum?'

The only Chief Constable in captivity to read philosophy.

Kersey was looking out of the window. 'You spoke too soon; we've got visitors: Ella with a cameraman in tow.'

Ella Bunt: freelance crime reporter, thirty-five, a redhead and a militant feminist. ('We're not equal, we're better! I've proved it in bed and out.') Ella owed her husky voice to cigarettes and her complexion to whisky but she rarely missed out on a story and few editors could afford to ignore her. Wycliffe knew her of old and between them there was a love-hate relationship.

Kersey met her at the door. 'No pets! Leave him outside, Ella.'

The cameraman said: 'I'll be about.'

Ella sat opposite Wycliffe. 'Had a good Christmas with your lawyer friend? You won't mind if I smoke?'

'Make yourself at home, Ella.'

She blew smoke across the table. 'Awkward for you; finding yourself a house guest with the principal suspects, but I gather you moved out. Sensible! Warm in here.' She stood up and slipped off a fleece-lined leather jacket which smelt of goat. 'It looks dicey for The Sheriff. I wouldn't be surprised if this started a whole lot of rumours. And him all set for office. I've been doing my homework on the Lemarque/Bateman set-up. It's a wonder he survived that and kept his seat; he may not be so lucky this time. Of course he must have friends. Lemarque probably felt he'd been left holding the shitty end and maybe he was intending to get his own back.'

Wycliffe said: 'Don't let me spoil things for you, Ella, but it was Mrs Lemarque who was shot.'

'I know. Odd that. Something went wrong somewhere. So you've found the girl; what does she have to say?'

'Very little.'

'Can I talk to her?'

'It's not up to me; her aunt is down.'

'Where's her papa?'

'I was hoping you might help me to find him. I expect you've had the hand-outs about him and his van.'

'And that's all you've got on him?'

'Scout's honour.'

'No reported sightings?'

'Not one.'

'There you are then! It would make more sense than killing her, don't you think?'

'I try not to. Look, Ella, if you haven't got any questions I can answer, why not let us get on with it in our own bumbling fashion?'

'I want background.'

Wycliffe made a broad gesture. 'It's all out there. Take what you want.'

'Very funny! How about a couple of shots inside the Lemarque house?'

'Not a chance, but you can take all you want outside.'

'Thank you for nothing. What about the gun?'

'A .38 automatic.'

'Have you found it?'

'No.' Wycliffe stood up. 'You want the human interest angle, Ella. Go and talk to Evadne Penrose, 6, Wesley Terrace, but don't say I sent you. Friend of the dead woman, astrologer extraordinaire, and probably glad of somebody to talk to.'

'Are you fobbing me off?'

'I wouldn't dare.'

She got up and struggled into her jacket. 'I hope not. Anyway, I'll be around for a bit.'

When she had gone Wycliffe said: 'Ella's nobody's fool but she and Evadne deserve each other, don't you think?'

Among other memoranda that morning there was one from C.R.O. in response to Kersey's enquiry about Marsden. Their reply was succinct: 'This subject has no criminal record.'

Kersey stared at the memo. 'I know I've come across that great baboon somewhere, in a nick and on the wrong side of the counter, but I'm damned if I can remember—' He broke off in a triumphant *eureka* moment of recall: 'I've got it! I was a wooden top in Paddington on a six-month stint as part of an exchange programme; finding out about the other half. Marsden was nicked by the art forgery boys. I wasn't on the case but a mate of mine in C.I.D. was roped in to help with the leg work and it opened his eyes to what goes on in the art racket.'

'Did it come to court?'

'I can't remember; I may not have heard because it was towards the end of my time. He can't have been convicted otherwise he'd have form.'

Wycliffe was putting on his overcoat. 'Follow it up. I'm going prospecting.'

'Around Mennear Bal; I thought you might.'

Wycliffe drove out of the village in the direction of Pendeen. Beyond the Mechanics' Institute the cottages petered out, and the road ran between dry-stone hedges with an occasional dwarf hawthorn, sculptured like a fox's brush by the salt winds. After half-a-mile the hedge on the right gave way to an open space with a few cottages and ramshackle bungalows scattered at random among patches of rough grass. Several tracks led off in the general direction of the sea. He pulled off the road and got out. Three or four old bangers were dotted about, parked or dumped, and a stocky young man with curly black hair was working on one of them. He did not look up though Wycliffe came to stand within a couple of feet of him. The genuine Cornish article, unadulterated by foreign genes. He and his kind were already established in the county when the upstart Celts arrived and ever since they've been plagued by strangers.

'Good morning! Is this Mennear Bal?'

'Used to be.' Still without looking up.

'Which of these tracks leads to the cliff?'

'They all do.'

'Can I drive out there?'

'Tha's up to you; whether yer bothered about yer suspension.'

Wycliffe was and decided to walk; he chose the first of the tracks he came to. The ground was flat (an elevated plain of marine denudation, geologists said) and dotted with ruined buildings, heaps of rubble, and the occasional inhabited cottage. Between St Ives and Cape Cornwall copper and tin mines were once strung out along the coast like beads on a string, now only one is working; the others are in ruins, or have disappeared altogether or, like the quoits, graves, standing stones, and courtyard houses of prehistory, are being preserved because of their archaeological interest.

Mennear Bal was a ruin, rather a collection of ruins; a chimney stack or two, crumbling engine houses, roofless sheds, and intimations of what once had been a maze of arsenic flues. In the sunshine and the silence it was hard to imagine scores of bal maidens and buddle boys thronging the site, smashing ore, feeding the stamps, and doing homage to their employer for fivepence a day. Even harder to imagine bands of happy campers paying their dues to Bateman and Lemarque. Wycliffe had heard the expression, 'cheerful as a knacked bal', now he knew what it meant.

But a quarter-of-a-mile ahead the sea sparkled under the sun, an enduring backdrop. Wycliffe's track joined others and eventually he was walking along a broad path, parallel with the sea; on his left the grass curved smoothly and swiftly away to the cliff edge and a drop of more feet than he cared to think about. At a short distance off-shore a St Ives boat was cruising, perhaps her first chance to put out following the storm and the fog. Far out a container ship forged her way up-channel.

The track, made up of coarse mineral waste from the spoil heaps, was peppered with pot-holes and there were broad puddles, but scarcely any mud. He had hoped to find traces of Lemarque's van but he was disappointed. The man had probably stopped some-where along the track to brood like Moses on the promised land; though, again like Moses, he would have needed all his entrepreneurial optimism to see milk and honey in the prospect. Which did not mean that he would be in a mood to go home and shoot his wife.

Wycliffe continued walking until he was leaving the mine workings behind. At this point, just before the track narrowed to a footpath, he noticed furrows in the grass bordering the track on the sea side, and the furrows were of a kind that might have been made by the wheels of a car or van. The slope to the cliff edge was steep, too steep and slippery for a man to risk climbing down, and the furrows were cut into the mounded grass where it met the path; he could distinguish three of them clearly with the hint of a fourth. Once over that mound nothing could have stopped any vehicle hurtling down.

As he examined the surface of the track he could see that the ballast had been disturbed by a swirling movement of the kind made by skidding back wheels. He worked back along the way he had come for about two hundred yards, examining the ground carefully as he went, and found what he had missed before: two wheel-ruts where the back wheels of the vehicle had dug in as a consequence of rapid acceleration. The story seemed to tell itself. Someone in a vehicle which was either stationary or moving very slowly, suddenly accelerated, steered for the end of the track where it narrowed, swerved off down the grassy slope and over the cliff.

An accident? An improbable one.

Was it Lemarque's van which had left those tell-tale signs? More than likely. It would explain why the van had not been spotted, or Lemarque either. But he had to bear in mind the possibility that one of the inhabitants of Mennear Bal had finally tired of his vintage jalopy and hoisted it over the cliff. The authorities might frown on such practices but there was a maverick strain in these people who shared their ancestry with Bishop Trelawny.

He looked around for any position where he might

get a view of the cliff face but there was none, then he spotted a place where the grassy slope to the cliff edge looked less steep and less slippery, where the grass grew in hummocks which offered some sort of foothold. He stepped gingerly off the track, wedging his foot against one of the hummocks; it felt precarious and immediately the edge seemed much nearer and the sea a very long way down. He decided to sacrifice dignity to relative stability and got down on all fours. Working backwards, groping with his feet, and clutching at the mounds of grass with his hands, he moved crabwise down the slope feeling like a fly on the wall.

'Police Chief Killed in Fall from Cliff. Foul Play Not Excluded', nor idiocy neither. He was as near the edge as he dared go; now he had to wriggle round so that he could look over. The grass was short near the edge where soil was almost non-existent and his knees suffered painful encounters with protruding rocks, but he managed it. He peered over the edge and received a dizzy impression of dark blue water and a lacy edge of foam; he was never at ease when his feet were higher than his head but he collected his wits and realized that the cliff was not sheer to the sea. Half-way down, perhaps eighty feet or so, there was a substantial abutment, presumably the result of a landslip, and lodged on this broad ledge was a vehicle of some sort. It was lying on its side and all he could see of it was a front wheel and part of the bonnet in profile. He felt sure that it was Lemarque's Escort van but he could not be certain.

He crawled back with less difficulty than he had experienced getting down but when he stood once more on the old track he was trembling; his trousers were covered in greenish slime and his right hand was bleeding from a graze. He tidied himself as best he could and found his way through the maze of tracks to where he had left his car.

*

They studied the map, identified the tiny inlet where Lemarque's car might be, and agreed on a map reference. Wycliffe arranged for the cliff track to be sealed off and for a scene-of-crime team under Fox to make a meticulous search of the whole stretch. Prospects were poor after the storm on Christmas Eve but it had to be done.

Then a telephone call to the Naval Air Station and an accommodating Lieutenant Commander. Yes, they had an Air Sea Rescue helicopter in the neighbourhood on a training flight; no problem to have a look-see. Call you back. That simple.

Kersey said: 'If Lemarque is at the bottom of that cliff he must have shot his wife before he went joy-riding among the mine dumps.'

'If he shot his wife, what you say seems reasonable.'

Outside a car engine cut, a door slammed, and they heard Alice Devlin's voice talking to Potter. She came in, crisp and fresh and smelling expensive.

'I hope I've done the right thing; I've allowed myself to be persuaded or bulldozed. That young lady knows her own mind and I had little option. I've left her with the Bishops.' She slipped off a suede shoulder bag and put it on the table.

'Do sit down. This is Detective Inspector Kersey. I don't suppose you want to risk police coffee? . . . I don't blame you.'

'She asked me to take her there. I suppose it was only natural she should want to see them and they her, the two families were very close before Alain got into trouble. But I must admit I was surprised when they asked her to stay at Mynhager and she agreed – just like that; no argument, no discussion. Of course I don't know her very well but it seemed out of character. I think they were a bit surprised too.'

'Who did you see?'

'Ernest, is it? And his two sisters; the old man, and a lad called Paul. Early on we were joined by Gerald

130

Bateman M.P.' She smiled. 'I hadn't realized we were moving in the corridors of power; the name didn't click at first.'

'Did she give you any idea why she is so anxious to stay with the Bishops?'

'Only that she knew them well and that she had spent a good deal of time in the house. She feels closer to them than to me, so I suppose it's all right for the time being.'

She sat back in her chair. 'No news of Alain?'

'I'm afraid not. I assume you are doing the necessary to put other members of the family on your side in the picture, but we are concerned about the Lemarques. We've no contact. I don't suppose you can help?'

She shook her head. 'All I know is that Alain's father came over with the Free French during the war.'

Wycliffe tested the water. 'I suppose you realize that one possibility is that your sister was killed by her husband?'

'Of course I've thought of that.'

'You think it credible?'

A lengthy pause. 'I simply don't know. I've see Alain three or four times and then only briefly. He struck me as being very fond of Jane and perhaps over anxious to please her.'

'I don't want to put any pressure on Francine but I suspect she could tell us more than she has.'

Pursed lips. 'You could be right but if she's keeping anything from you, she hasn't confided in me. I've been kept very much in my place as a visiting aunt of slender acquaintance. Not that I blame her, poor child.'

She picked up her bag. 'I suppose it might be useful if I was around for a day or two?'

'I'm sure it would be.'

'Good! Apart from anything else, Francine may need a shoulder to weep on, though I doubt it.'

They talked briefly of the inquest, of the need for a disposal certificate and of the funeral which must come sometime.

Sensible woman!

On cue, as the Sierra was driven off, the Lieutenant Commander called: 'I think we've located your motor; the chaps have just radioed in. Something the worse for wear I gather. Ford Escort van, grey; registration number: Oscar Foxtrot Quebec One Three Four Papa. Snap?'

'Snap.'

'They couldn't get close enough to read the engine number. Sorry!' Funny man. 'No sign of any occupant; one door missing, the other hanging, three wheels adrift and the bodywork suffering from multiple contusions.'

'Any ideas on accessibility?'

'I enquired. Our chaps say the vehicle is caught on a sort of abutment, a land slip, about eighty feet above the tide line. They reckon the base of the cliff is uncovered at low water but it sounds as though you'll need a lift if you want to recover.'

'Any chance of your people taking it on?'

'Why not? It would be a useful exercise. I'd have to get clearance but I think that could be arranged if your lot are prepared to pay the piper.'

'Just one more thing: we want the driver of the van. He may or may not have gone over with it but we have to start looking.'

'Did all this happen before or after the force 10 on Saturday?'

'Shortly before. I wondered if you could manage a low-level sweep or two while your chaps are in the air?'

'Can do, but I don't hold out much hope of finding anything. The van didn't go all the way, but he probably did and it's unlikely that he's still in one piece.'

'Thanks. I'm notifying Coastguard and I'll keep in touch.'

Kersey said: 'I agree that we want the van and having the fly-boys lift it is probably the best way. But we want Lemarque more. If we don't find him the case folds.'

Wycliffe glanced at his watch: 'Eleven-fifteen. Just

over five hours of something like daylight. If the tide is right and there's a boat available we could take a look.'

'That "we" – is it the royal, the editorial, or does it just mean you and me?'

'In this instance it means you.'

'I was afraid of that. Marine exploration is not my thing.'

'It broadens the mind.'

'And empties the stomach.'

'If Lemarque did go overboard with the van, the longer the delay the less chance we have of finding him in identifiable pieces if at all. Get on to Coastguard and see if you can arrange for the inshore lifeboat. Take one of our chaps along who's grasped the rudiments of being able to stand upright on a slippery rock. I don't want any mountaineering; if it comes to that we'll bring in the professionals. And don't be defeatist; it's like a millpond out there.'

'Until you're on it.'

Kersey reached for the telephone.

'Do it next door.'

Alone, Wycliffe pared his nails, brooded, and tried to order his thoughts. Whether they admitted it or not, all concerned seemed to assume that Lemarque had killed his wife. And it was a reasonable assumption, given support by the finding of the van. Lemarque had taken his van to Mennear Bal and committed suicide by driving over the cliff. A believable reaction to a crime of passion. Remorse, promptly followed by a dramatic and final expiation. But Wycliffe had already questioned the passion, and all but settled for premeditation. So, a different sequel: After shooting his wife, Lemarque had ditched the van at Mennear Bal to create the impression that he had killed himself, and was now on the run.

But there were flaws, possibly fatal to both notions: Franks believed that Jane Lemarque had died between four and eight, and it now seemed that the dead woman had been talking to the ineffable Evadne at four-thirty.

133

A fat boy sitting on the low wall of the churchyard was watching him solemnly and intently through the window. Wycliffe winked at him and immediately felt guilty when he saw the shocked look on the lad's face. One more recruit to the ranks of disillusioned youth.

Where was he? A third alternative – was there such a thing? Anyway, a third possibility: Lemarque had ditched his van before killing his wife. Improbable but not impossible. It would mean that he had really planned the killing in cold blood.

At least he had clarified his own thoughts. The thing now was to recover the van and find Lemarque, alive or dead.

By dint of persuasion, warnings, even threats, he obtained authority from the mandarins in Accounts to employ an R.N.A.S. helicopter for the recovery of Lemarque's van.

'Is it absolutely essential to the chain of evidence? Is there no other way in which recovery could be effected? By boat, for example? Have you considered recovery by sea? Surely there is a well known climbing school and cliff rescue centre in that neighbourhood – couldn't they do what is necessary? You do realize that helicopters are fiendishly expensive to hire? I mean even more expensive than fixed-wing aircraft.'

'I suppose a fixed-wing aircraft might scoop the thing up at a hundred and twenty knots provided it didn't hit the cliff face.'

'You are being facetious, Chief Superintendent. I am only trying to do my job.'

'Aren't we all?'

Probably the Lieutenant Commander would have complementary difficulties with his administration, but at last the financial and logistical problems would be solved and arrangements made. Too late for that day.

Wycliffe arranged for the house-to-house to be extended to the cottages at Mennear Bal. Others might have heard or seen as much or more than the girl at The Tributers.

He had a snack lunch alone in the bar. Ella Bunt was there, sharing a table with Marsden. They seemed to be getting on well together.

As Wycliffe passed their table on his way out, Ella looked up. 'Thanks for the tip; you did me proud. I'll remember it.'

Thanks from a reporter must sound ominous in the ears of any policeman. Wycliffe wondered what she had cooked up with Evadne Penrose and the painter.

It was not Kersey with his inshore lifeboat who found Lemarque but a St Ives boatman, catching up on the wind and fog. Lemarque's body, drifting just below the surface of the water, nuzzled his bows, slid silently along the port side and would have cleared his stern had he not seen it, cut his engine and grabbed it with a boathook. He secured a rope round the legs and towed it back because it was difficult to get aboard without assistance. In any case he didn't fancy the job.

Arrived in harbour, he telephoned the police, and Sergeant Curtis came down to inspect his catch. Curtis recognized Lemarque, the proportions rather than the features, and reported to Wycliffe.

'The left side of his neck and the right side of his face are badly damaged, sir. The fish have been busy but there's more to it than that. He was shot, or he shot himself.'

Wycliffe left the duty officer to make the routine notifications and drove to St Ives.

St Ives: 'a pretty good town and grown rich by the fishing trade' – Daniel Defoe, a one-man K.G.B., reporting to Speaker Harley in 1702. Now it has grown richer, not on fish but on tourists and the reputations of dead painters. But, despite its prosperity, for seven or eight months of the twelve its streets are empty and many of its shops, cafés and restaurants are closed. Wycliffe arrived in the after-glow of sunset, the town in shadow, the bay lambent and still. A few figures on the quay, motionless in silhouette, standing near a little mound of plastic sheeting.

Curtis was there. 'This is Jack Martin; he brought him in. Found him floating in the lee of Clodgy Point.'

A short stout man in a sailor's cap and a duffel coat held out a firm plump hand.

The plastic sheet was lifted. Lemarque wore an anorak, zipped to the neck, brownish trousers, no shoes. The shoes belonging to Lemarque at the cottage were all non lace-ups, so it was likely that those he had been wearing had fallen off. His socks had been nibbled at in several places revealing sometimes pallid skin, sometimes abraded flesh. But Wycliffe's attention focused on the face and neck. No doubt that Lemarque had shot himself or been shot; a bullet had entered the neck just below the jaw-bone and made its exit high up the face on the other side. The wound of entry had been enlarged and made more ragged after death, presumably by the fish. It would be up to the pathologist and the ballistics experts to decide, but there seemed no obvious reason why the original bullet wound could not have been self-inflicted.

He was wearing a wrist watch, and the metal bracelet had cut into the swollen flesh. The glass of the watch, badly cracked, must have let in water but the hands were undamaged and showed twelve minutes past three. There was a day/date inset but Wycliffe could not read the display; the experts would have no difficulty.

'All right, you can cover him up.'

The police surgeon arrived, a man of few words, he made a cursory examination and left. A van brought the plastic shell in which the body would be conveyed to the mortuary, there to await the arrival of Dr Franks for the post mortem. Wycliffe spent a few minutes with Curtis in the local station then drove up the long steep hill out of the town on his way back to Mulfra.

It was almost dark but far out the sea gleamed in the last remnants of the day, and the sky was faintly flushed with red; the promise of a fine tomorrow.

So Lemarque was dead; shot through the neck and head, as his wife had been. Suicide or murder? The positions of the wounds of entry and exit were consistent with either. Lemarque could have driven his van over the grassy hump which bordered the cliff track and in those seconds while it was hurtling to the cliff edge, he could have shot himself. It was not especially uncommon for determined suicides to do a belt-and-braces job: shooting themselves in the instant of jumping off a bridge; taking poison, then drowning themselves. There was even a case on record of a man who hanged himself and cut his throat.

The van had landed on a projecting platform of rock well down the cliff face and the shock of impact would almost certainly have burst open the doors so that a man in the driving seat might well have been thrown clear and continued on down to the water. Memo: check on tides. Was Lemarque left-handed?

But now came the crunch: was it likely that Lemarque had carefully planned and executed his wife's murder, then committed suicide? More than that, if the time by Lemarque's watch was an indication of the time of his death then there was no way in which he could have been his wife's killer.

Adding it all up, Wycliffe was being forced to face the possibility of a double murder and if that was the case he was literally without a clue where to begin; they were up the creek without a paddle.

When he arrived back at the van Kersey was plaintive. 'Have you ever been out in one of those inflatables? It's like putting to sea on a couple of salami sausages; the damn thing keeps bobbing up and down like a cork.

Under the cliff you catch the swell going in and bouncing back. My stomach feels like an overworked yo-yo. And all for nothing! Some other guy a mile or two up the coast beats us to it.'

Joseph had spent most of the day in his room, a good deal of it looking out of the window. He had watched an Air Sea Rescue helicopter fluttering up and down, following the configuration of the coastline, at or below cliff-top height. Then, later, the inshore lifeboat had taken over, nosing into the coves and inlets, lost to sight for long periods but always emerging to round the next promontory. It was not a novel routine, it happened in the tourist season when a too confident swimmer or some idiot on an air-bed got swept out to sea, and something similar occurred in the winter when they were searching for drums of toxic chemicals washed overboard from a freighter, or for bodies from a wrecked ship. But today's activity had worried Joseph because he could not get it out of his head that they were looking for Lemarque.

Now it was dark and the search had either ended or been postponed.

He could not focus the reason for his unease. Jane Lemarque had been murdered, apparently by her husband; a tragedy in any circumstances but the more stark because it concerned people one knew, people with whom there had been intimacy and friendship. But Joseph had never been a sentimentalist and now he had reached an age when, like any sensible man, he had cultivated a nodding acquaintance with death and the habit of distancing himself from grief.

His disquiet stemmed from an illogical conviction that the tragedy was not yet played out, that it would move nearer home. He looked round at his books, at his photographs and paintings, at the room which sustained him in his old age and for the first time felt insecure. Absurdly, he associated this foreboding with the arrival of the girl. That morning she had moved in . . .

He got up from his chair and in a single irritable movement swept the curtains over the window so that the wooden rings rattled together. 'God! I'm going soft in the head!'

A tap on the door and Ernest came in. 'Are you all right?' Concerned.

The old man snapped at him. 'Of course I'm all right! Why shouldn't I be?'

Ernest, not reassured, knew better than to argue. 'Wycliffe has been on the phone.'

'They've found Lemarque.'

'How on earth do you know?'

'Dead?'

'Yes.'

'Drowned?'

'Shot, but Wycliffe didn't give details. All I know is that his van was found half-way down the cliff at Mennear Bal and his body was picked up floating in the sea. He wanted to know if Lemarque was left-handed.'

'He wasn't, was he?'

'No. I suppose they're thinking of suicide, presumably after killing Jane.'

The old man made an irritable movement. 'All nice and tidy! So it's as good as over; soon everybody can pack up and go home.'

Ernest's astonishment was obvious. 'I don't understand.'

'You wouldn't! Has anybody told the girl?'

'Vee is with her now.'

'Yes, well, we shall see.'

Caroline came into the room from the kitchen, Virginia from the hall. The family, apart from the two sisters, was already seated round the table which was set with nine places.

139

Joseph sat at the head of the table, waiting.

Somebody said: 'Is she coming down, Vee?'

'I think so; she wants to change first.'

Joseph thought: Vee's pleasure in life consists in persuading people to do what they don't want to. The born schoolteacher.

The high, gloomy room, panelled by its nineteenth-century architect, was dimly lit by electric bracket lamps in the form of fake candles. Family portraits by indifferent Victorian and Edwardian painters were flattered by the poor lighting.

Paul was staring at his empty plate and fiddling with his soup spoon. 'She won't let me talk to her.'

'You must give her time, Paul.'

Too easily hurt. Paul had the Bishop looks, something of the Bishop temperament, but not the Bishop hide.

Joseph's feelings of unease increased, he sensed that they were moving towards a crisis. A premonition? He did not believe in such things. Or did he? At seventy-five he realized that all his life he had adopted postures to defend himself against a corroding sense of insecurity. These postures had fathered his beliefs. Was this true of others? Of Bateman, for instance? If it was, did he know it?

All Joseph knew at this moment was that he was listening to meaningless verbal exchanges between members of his family while underneath . . .

Virginia took her place beside Paul; something more than aunty affection there. She was explaining: 'When I went to her door I could hear her voice and I thought someone must be with her but she was alone. She was sitting in the dark by the window with the curtains drawn back. I said: "I thought you were talking to someone", and she said: "I was, I was talking to Blackie."'

Joseph was impelled to question. 'Blackie?'

'The black-faced doll she's had since she was a baby.'

Caroline amended: 'I gave her that doll on her third birthday.'

140

Stella reached for a bread roll and started to crumble it on her side plate. Joseph thought: Stella can't wait for her food. At least I haven't become greedy in my old age. Not for food, anyway. Stella was saying something: 'I used to talk to my dolls when George was away. I had thirty of them from every part of India.'

Bateman made his contribution: 'She's had a terrible shock, poor girl. How is she taking it, Vee?'

'I really don't know. She seemed strange rather than grieved but you can't . . . ' She broke off as Francine entered the room.

Joseph drew in his breath. Francine wore a blue dress that was almost a gown; her red-gold hair was gathered into a coil on the top of her head displaying her long youthful neck. Beautiful! Necks and ankles are the erogenous zones for a young woman. The eighteenth century understood this: display the neck, titillate with the ankles. Women have lost the art of titillation.

Joseph felt compelled to pay homage. 'I'm very glad you've come down, my dear.'

'Thank you, daddy Jo.' It was the name she had called him from the time she had learned to talk. God alone knew why.

Caroline said: 'I'll tell Ada we're ready.' She came back a minute or two later, with Ada carrying a large tureen of soup. When it had been served, they settled down to their meal. No one could think of anything to say and as the silence lengthened so the tension seemed to rise. Several times Ernest cleared his throat as though to speak but changed his mind.

Joseph thought: He's on edge. He keeps looking at the girl. Covert glances, as though he's anxious not to be seen to look at her. If I didn't know him I'd think it was lust. What's the matter with him? There is a streak of weakness, a flaw, which makes him unpredictable. Even as a child . . .

Then there was Gerald, nephew and son-in-law, yet Joseph had always found it difficult to think of him as

141

one of the family. He sat bolt upright, staring straight ahead, going through the motions of drinking the soup like an automaton. He was good at it, never spilling a drop. Joseph thought: He knows; his politician's antennae are signalling trouble ahead.

Caroline was uneasy too. She was of coarser stuff than her sister but more perceptive. Vee lived on the surface of things, responsive to every wind that blew, but Carrie was aware of the undertow of life, which was probably why she needed to drink. Neither of the girls had turned out like their mother.

Joseph felt a warmth behind the eyes, remembering his wife. Ursula. Her name still had the power to move him. He was trying to recall how she had looked when they first met. Ursula at seventeen . . . 1927; talkies and the slow fox-trot; Rex Whistler at the Tate, Aldous Huxley, Evelyn Waugh, Virginia Woolf . . .

His gaze rested once more on Francine and he was startled. Why had he never realized it before? Or was he imagining it now? He had never seen the girl with her hair up until tonight . . .

Vee was helping Ada to serve the main course. Spare ribs of beef in a marinade: one of his favourite dishes but his appetite had gone. He was watching Francine. She had small helpings but she ate with prim and delicate efficiency. Apart from Stella she seemed to be the only one untroubled by the silence.

After the meal they went into the drawing-room for coffee. Conversation, which began around the percolator, continued when they sat down; the spell of silence had been broken. They talked about the weather; the mild spell, the prospect of January frosts and, inevitably, someone quoted: 'As the days begin to lengthen, the cold begins to strengthen.'

Francine sat in one of the smaller armchairs and Virginia squatted on the floor at her side. Virginia was a great floor squatter. Joseph could see her lips moving almost continuously, provoking only occasional

142

responses from the girl then, abruptly, during a lull in other conversation, Francine's voice became clearly audible to all: 'The man they found this afternoon was not my father!' Her voice was taut and brittle. She got to her feet, looked about her uncertainly, then hurried from the room. Virginia went after her and Paul, very pale, followed them.

Bateman said: 'Poor child!'

Caroline looked round at the others. 'Do you think I should go up?' And when no one answered decided to stay where she was.

Ernest sat in his chair, staring with absorbed attention at his empty coffee cup.

Stella went on with her knitting as though nothing had happened and the ultimate platitude was left to Ada. 'She'll be better after a good cry.'

CHAPTER NINE

Wednesday morning; Christmas Day plus three. A second fine day in a row, an achievement for late December. When it happens a Cornishman begins to wonder if something has gone wrong with the Divine Order. Wycliffe and Kersey arrived at the Incident Van at half-past eight after breakfasting with Alice Devlin. Alice had decided to stay on until after the joint funeral of her sister and brother-in-law. 'But I must slip up to Bristol for one or two nights to deal with things. My husband is in Brussels.'

The newspapers were on Wycliffe's table and Ella Bunt had made the front page of one of the tabloids under an 'exclusive' tag.

Former Partner of Law and Order M.P. Missing Alain Lemarque, recently released from prison after serving a sentence for fraud, is wanted for questioning in connection with the murder of his wife, Jane, at their Cornish cottage on Christmas Eve.

Gerald Bateman M.P., known to his colleagues as 'The Sheriff', and tipped for office in the forthcoming government re-shuffle, was a partner in the Lemarque enterprises before they ran into trouble; trouble which culminated in Lemarque being sentenced to two years for fraud. Mr Bateman, when he is not at Westminster or in his constituency, lives across the valley from the Lemarques with his in-laws, the Bishop family who, for generations, have been lawyers in the neighbouring town of Penzance.

By coincidence, the head of the area C.I.D. Chief Superintendent Charles Wycliffe, now in charge of the inquiry, was staying with the Bishops at the time of the tragedy. It is understood that he has since removed himself to the local inn . . .

Wycliffe muttered: 'It could have been worse I suppose.'

At nine o'clock Dr Franks telephoned his preliminary report on the autopsy.

'Obviously the man was shot not drowned but his body must have got into the sea very shortly after death . . . He was shot through the left side of his neck with an upward inclination of the weapon and the bullet emerged higher up on the other side. A repeat performance of his wife's killing except that the gun was probably held close to the skin if not actually touching . . . Difficult to be quite sure about that because the wound of entry was enlarged through being nibbled by fish. On the evidence of the body alone I'd say it could have been either suicide or murder.'

'He wasn't left-handed.'

'Ah! I was coming to that, but it doesn't make much difference. If he was steering the van to the edge of the cliff when he fired he would have had his right hand on the wheel. If he didn't steer the van Sod's Law would see to it that the thing tipped over and stuck half-way down the slope without reaching the edge. Very frustrating for a chap all set to make a dramatic exit. And you must know that it isn't difficult to fire a gun with your left hand if you don't have to aim it.'

Wycliffe was watching Kersey light a cigarette. Automatically he reached into his right-hand jacket pocket where for twenty-five years he had kept his pipe; it was no longer there. Frustration, and an empty feeling akin to hunger. He muttered angrily to himself: 'I'm like an infant deprived of its dummy!' Absurdly, his manner

145

towards Franks became noticeably sharper: 'The real question is whether Lemarque was in the van when the shot was fired. For all we know it was pushed empty over the cliff.'

Franks was amused. 'Fascinating! The idea of this bloke pushing his van over the cliff, then taking a running jump after it, shooting himself on the way. A bit whimsical, don't you think?'

A rueful laugh. 'Go to hell! What I'm really saying is that the evidence of his watch makes it less likely that he killed himself. Why should he if he hadn't killed his wife?'

'Search me! Motive is not my problem, Charles. I can tell you though that if he was shot in the van, whether he did it himself or not, I'd expect a fair old mess of spattered blood and soft tissue. At least you'll be able to check on that when they hoist the van aboard. And one more thing you can chew over in the silent watches: when we were undressing him we came across plant fragments caught between his anorak and his shirt. They included two dried up, papery little bladder-like objects. My assistant, who knows about such things, says they are the calyces of the sea campion. It seems those often survive on the flower stalk through the winter; and the sea campion, according to her, is found on the grassy slopes of the cliffs. So it looks as though our friend might have had a roll in the grass before finally taking off. How's that for service beyond the call of duty?'

Wycliffe had to admit that Franks had given him more than he could reasonably expect in a preliminary report. And on balance it seemed to strengthen the case for believing that Lemarque had been murdered. A double murder.

With any luck they would have the wrecked van available for examination later in the morning. The weather was calm, the sea placid, visibility excellent. Ideal flying weather, and there might not be another such day for weeks. The van would be lifted by the helicopter on to a truck parked on the cliff-top, then taken to a police garage for forensic examination.

Detailed arrangements had been made and it was all systems go.

Kersey said: 'This case, like Topsy, jes growed! From a silly girl going a.w.o.l. to a couple of homicides.'

'And we've next to nothing to go on. I want you to get in touch with Rosemergy Minerals and find out the state of play between them and Lemarque over the Mennear Bal site, also how far Bateman is known to be involved.'

Kersey had been turning over the latest reports.

'Anything new?'

'What there is comes from Mennear Bal. Two more sightings of the grey Escort van being driven in the direction of the cliff at around three o'clock on Christmas Eve. More interesting: there's a statement from a man out walking his dog . . . ' Kersey searched for the page. 'Alamein Montgomery Choak, aged forty-two; he would be with a name like that, poor bastard! He was walking along the track at the cliff edge when he came across the van, parked unattended. He actually passed it.'

'Interesting! What time was that?'

'He says about half-past three.'

'Say, an hour before Jane Lemarque telephoned Evadne Penrose. Was Lemarque alive or dead at that time?'

Kersey put the report back in its file. 'Good question. If we go by his watch he was already dead.'

Wycliffe got up from his seat. 'I shall be at Mynhager for the next hour or so.'

'Anything particular in mind?'

'Just a fishing expedition.'

Outside in the sunshine he decided to walk to Mynhager. It was part of the folk-lore of headquarters that the chief never drove if he could walk because walking was quicker. The truth was that he disliked being driven, and when he drove he rarely clocked much over 50. Anyway it was a nice day, almost like summer, though tomorrow or the day after could bring a tempest or a frost. At the moment women stood in their doorways, and little knots of people were gossiping outside the shops and on the sunny side of the street.

Wycliffe turned down by the pub, preoccupied. If there had in fact been a double murder, why had anyone wanted to kill Lemarque and his wife? Bateman and the Bishops had been on more or less intimate terms with them for nearly twenty years so Mynhager was the obvious place to start. But there was more to it than that.

An ancient Mini passed him and came to a stop a little way ahead, by the painter's cottage. A blonde young woman got out, came round to the back, opened the boot and lifted out a large travelling case, obviously empty. Marsden's woman friend come to collect her belongings? She slammed the boot shut and went into the cottage. As he drew level Wycliffe could see the two of them through the window of the living-room.

He plodded on along the track until he rounded the bend and came in sight of Mynhager. Even in the sunshine the house stood out starkly against the sky. He went round to the front and rang the bell. To his surprise it was answered by Francine. She look strained, hollow-eyed and pale, but her manner was not unwelcoming. She even managed a smile.

'You'd better come into the drawing-room; I don't know who you want to see . . .'

Sunshine flooded through the big window so that the fire in the grate was dimmed by its brilliance but the room itself appeared more tatty than ever, the holly looked sad, the paper chains, pathetic.

She picked up a large photograph album from one of the settees. 'Shall I tell them you're here?'

'Family photographs?'

'I was looking at them.'

'Do you mind if I look?'

He sat on the settee, took the book from her hands, and turned the pages while she stood over him. He had the impression that she was not displeased.

The usual family snapshots, mainly of groups of people either posed formally on the terrace or snapped casually on picnics or boating trips. None of them was recent.

'Most of them were taken before I was born.'

He stopped at a lively group taken in a sandy cove. It was dated 1967. She said: 'Mamma Bishop took most of these. I used to call her that; she died when I was five.' The men, Joseph among them, wore trunks or shorts, the girls, bikinis.

'That's my mother, a year before I was born.' Even in the snapshot the girl stood out as a quite exceptional beauty; she was laughing and seemed to be putting up token resistance to an attempt by a boisterous Bateman to place a garland of seaweed round her neck. All the others wore crowns and garlands of seaweed while Ernest had contrived a kilt for himself and stood in regal pose holding a paddle in place of a trident. Lemarque crouched frog-like on the sand beside a slimmer, almost lithe Caroline, who was adding something to his crown. Virginia watched her sister with obvious disapproval.

In later snapshots Francine was there, first as a baby in the arms of one or the other, later as a toddler, then as a trim, self-possessed little girl.

Wycliffe was puzzled, not by the snapshots but by Francine's satisfaction in his interest. It was as though she was saying: 'I want you to see how things were.'

Then the door opened and Bateman came in. His astonishment was obvious. 'Charles! I had no idea you were here. I've been wondering if we might be in touch. Of course I heard from Ernest . . .'

Francine said: 'If you want to talk I'll go somewhere else.' She went out, taking the album with her.

Bateman went on: 'I was greatly tempted to ring you

but I knew you wouldn't wish to be pestered until you were ready.'

What was it about this man which made Wycliffe bristle? Paleface speak with forked tongue but what politician does not? Nearer the truth, he had a barely conscious prejudice against those who swim where others sink; against chronic survivors. Totally irrational! Where would we be without them? But Wycliffe's sympathies were with the dinosaurs.

'Francine should have told me you were here but the poor child has had such a terrible shock.'

Bateman was casually elegant in corduroy slacks, checked Viyella shirt, cashmere cardigan, and custom-made house shoes. His broad dark moustache bristled in a perfect symmetry of graded lengths, and he was meticulously shaved. 'May I offer you something, Charles?'

'Thank you, no. It seems that Francine is taking an interest in times past.'

'Oh, the album . . . It belonged to my mother-in-law who never failed to record every family occasion. I don't know how Francine got hold of it.' Bateman dismissed the irrelevance and went on smoothly: 'I suppose we all knew in our hearts that this was the outcome to be expected but it still comes as a great shock.'

Wycliffe looked blank. 'What outcome? I don't understand.'

Bateman sat in an armchair, entirely relaxed. 'I merely meant that for a man like Alain there could be no other way. He must have been devastated by what he had done in a moment of madness.'

'You are assuming that he committed suicide after killing his wife?'

'What other explanation can there be?'

'We've reason to think that Lemarque predeceased his wife.'

Bateman's expression was one of total incredulity.

'Forgive me, but there must be some mistake! Who, other than Alain, could possibly have murdered Jane? Who had a motive? And why, if Jane was not dead at the time, did Alain kill himself? I can understand that a man facing the rebuilding of his life in middle age might feel intensely depressed but I have already told you that he was absorbed in a new venture which, knowing him, would certainly have restored his zest for life.'

Unconsciously Bateman was adopting his House of Commons tactics: beginning with an assertion and embroidering it with rhetorical questions.

By contrast, Wycliffe sounded casual. 'It's more than likely that Lemarque did not commit suicide.'

'I don't understand.'

'It's probable that he too was murdered.'

Bateman's hazel eyes studied Wycliffe intently for several seconds before he said: 'I find that quite incredible!'

At that moment there was a roar overhead and a helicopter appeared from over the house, flying low and following the line of the coast. At a distance of about half-a-mile it hovered, lost more height and vanished, hidden by the intervening headlands.

Both men were gazing out of the window. The sea stretched to the horizon, filling the framed picture except for a succession of headlands sheering away to the south-west. They could hear the pulsing of the helicopter's rotor blades but could not see it.

Wycliffe said: 'They're going to pick up Lemarque's van, what's left of it.'

He sensed a tremor of disquiet affecting them both. Was it that the tragedy seemed suddenly more real? But for Wycliffe at least the moment soon passed. Policemen, like doctors, deal in cases not tragedies.

He said: 'If this is a case of double murder, and I feel sure that it is, then we have to look outside the Lemarque family for a motive and for the killer. So far

151

we know almost nothing about them, while you and the Bishops have known them since before their marriage; naturally, we come to you for information.'

Bateman sat, finger tips matched; he spoke with careful deliberation: 'I can't believe that you are right but I will cooperate in any way I can and I'm sure the same goes for the rest of the family.'

Wycliffe's poker face would not have shamed Andrei Gromyko. 'For the moment I have only two or three questions: the first is probably the most important. From your knowledge of the Lemarques can you think of anyone with a grudge against them – against either or both?'

'No, I cannot.'

'I would like you to keep that question in mind; give yourself time to think about it. I suggest that you go back over the past few years which saw the break-up of your partnership and Lemarque's conviction for fraud. Later I may have to ask you for an account of your relations with Lemarque over those years and of his other contacts so far as they are known to you.'

'And your second question?' Bateman's cordiality had vanished.

'I need to know if Lemarque had any relatives in this country and whether he was in touch with them.'

'There, I'm afraid, I can't help you. Alain was always reticent about his family. To the best of my knowledge he came over here with his parents as a very young child, at the time of Dunkirk.'

'My next question is a simple matter of fact: when did you last see Lemarque or his wife?'

'I saw them both briefly on Christmas Eve.'

'At what time?'

Bateman was accustomed to being interrogated by TV interviewers about his politics, not by policemen about his private life; his distaste was obvious and his answer curt. 'At about two o'clock or perhaps a little later.'

'After your lunch here.'

'Certainly! You were our guest if you recollect.' Acid. 'I went for a walk and it occurred to me that it would be a friendly gesture to call on the Lemarques and try to cheer them up. At the same time I hoped to hear something more of the type of investment Alain had in mind.'

'And did you?'

'No. I had chosen a bad moment; how bad I've since realized. I could see that they were both under considerable strain and though they were perfectly civil it was obvious that I was anything but welcome at that particular time. Of course, as soon as I could decently extricate myself, I left. I wasn't in the house above five minutes.'

'Had you offered or been persuaded to back Lemarque's project with a large sum of money?'

Bateman looked startled. 'Certainly not! I didn't even know what he had in mind. All I did was to indicate a sympathetic interest.'

'What did you do when you left the cottage?'

A long slow look. 'I continued my walk.'

'Where did you go?'

This was too much for Bateman. 'Really! This begins to look like an interrogation.'

Wycliffe was coldly objective. 'I am asking you questions which seem proper in the circumstances but you don't have to answer them at this stage. As far as I know you were the last person to see Jane Lemarque alive apart from her husband and her killer. For that reason your evidence is important and you will be asked to make a written statement later.'

Bateman realized that he had made a tactical error, and acknowledged it with a thin smile. 'You are quite right. One has to get used to the idea of being a suspect but it is not something which comes easily.'

Wycliffe declined the bait. 'So where did you go?'

'I walked as far as Busullow and back through Morvah. I need plenty of exercise as I spend too much time at a desk.'

'Did you meet anyone?'

This was bloody-mindedness, but Bateman was not going to make the same mistake twice; he answered mildly: 'I suppose I must have done, especially walking back along the road but I don't remember anyone in particular.'

It was a reasonable answer.

Wycliffe had been watching Bateman, trying to sum him up, not because he had any real suspicion of the man but because he found the Bateman phenomenon interesting. A perceptive doctor, merely by looking at his patient, may spot the constitutional weakness which could mean future trouble in one or other of the organ systems of the body. Wycliffe tried to do something similar in his professional encounters though he was looking for moral weakness, for the heel of Achilles which made them vulnerable. In Bateman's case he thought he had found it. Bateman was a strong man but a vain one and his vanity laid him open on all fronts. He had to succeed or learn to despise the object of his failures.

Wycliffe wondered how he had come to terms with his marriage and his situation in the Bishop household.

'Just one more point.' Wycliffe drew from his pocket the envelope containing the newscutting, found amongst Lemarque's papers.

Bateman took it, read it, and handed it back. 'I don't understand. Where did you find that?'

Bateman had done his best to sound casual but Wycliffe was in no doubt that he was disturbed. 'You remember the occasion?'

'Of course I remember it. As you see I was guest speaker at the dinner.'

'Was Lemarque there?'

'As a guest, yes. Ernest invited him. The Lemarques were staying with us and it was an evening out for Alain.'

'Not for Jane?'

Bateman laughed. 'I'm afraid not; it was a stag party occasion. But why the interest?'

154

'These things crop up.'

Abruptly, the sound of the helicopter rotors, a muffled beat, increased in volume and the helicopter appeared, hovering clear of the headlands. Suspended from it by an invisible cord was a box-like contraption which could only have been the wreck of Lemarque's van. The helicopter moved a small distance inland, hovered, and again lost height. The transfer of its load to the waiting truck took place out of their sight, hidden by intervening higher ground. The truck would take the wreckage to the vehicle department at headquarters where Fox would examine it with an expert from Forensic.

Wycliffe got to his feet. He had learned something from Bateman, enough to be going on with. There would be time for more questions when he had more ammunition. 'Well, thank you for your co-operation; I'll arrange for someone to take your statement. Now, is your father-in-law at home?'

Bateman seemed surprised but made no comment. 'I think so. I'll take you to his room if you like.'

But in the hall they were waylaid by Aunt Stella who seemed to be doing sentry-go at the foot of the stairs. Aunt Stella in a blue silk blouse and a red skirt with the inevitable orange scarf.

'Ah, there you are, Mr Wycliffe! I've been waiting for you, but we can talk better in my room . . . '

Bateman shrugged and made his escape.

Aunt Stella had one of the bedrooms as a sitting-room. It was like a cave; the windows were draped with heavily patterned net; the decor, from the Bukhara carpet to the flock wallpaper and the upholstery of the Edwardian suite, was predominantly red. There were wall-cabinets chock full of bric-à-brac: ivory and ebony elephants of all sizes, multi-limbed Shivas in brass and bronze, various Buddhas cheek by jowl with Hindu gods and goddesses. Two massive radiators maintained a hothouse temperature.

'Do sit down, Chief Superintendent.' Stella's manner was confiding, even conspiratorial. 'Coffee to begin with I think.'

A coffee percolator on the hearth emitted jets of steam accompanied by vulgar noises and there was a tray with cups, a bowl of sugar, and a jug of cream on a low table near the window.

'As you can see, I have my own rooms.' She pointed to a door which broke the line of wall cabinets. 'My bedroom and bathroom are through there.'

The little red light on the percolator glowed, and its flatulence subsided. 'Ah, there we are! Black or white? . . . An oatmeal biscuit, Chief Superintendent?'

She had style, Wycliffe could imagine her, the pukka memsahib, presiding at tea parties, entertaining Indian big-wigs and high ranking civil servants to dinner. Always serene, always amusing and ready with that morsel of gossip, delicately spiced, which would titillate without vulgarity.

The preliminaries over, Aunt Stella said: 'I suppose keeping a gun without a permit is a serious offence?' She went on without waiting for an answer: 'They've probably told you that I'm weak in the head and that my memory is not what it was; that may be true, but I'm not bonkers, you understand.'

She looked at him, her little grey eyes alert for his reaction but he gave no sign. He sat in his chair, bolt upright, looking blank but not bored; his listening role. Over the years he had found that most people will talk more freely to a neutral listener, one who gives little indication of being either for or against, believing or unconvinced.

'They say I hide things then accuse people of having taken them; I assure you that I don't hide things – or not very often. I put them away and forget where I put them . . . ' A girlish laugh. 'Of course I sometimes say things just to shock them – silly things, I suppose, but even at my age one has to get some fun out of life. Now and then I'm quite wicked and I embarrass them in front of their friends, then they have to explain that I'm not quite right in the head.' She chuckled. 'But Ernest is so stuffy, worse than his father! And the two girls irritate me with their patronizing attitudes. I suppose it comes of having lived such sheltered lives.'

He felt sure that she was preparing the way for an admission which she regarded as more serious than possession of an unregistered firearm.

The room was so hot that he could feel the little beads of sweat forming on his forehead.

'About your gun, Mrs Burnett-Price . . .'

'I don't have a gun, Chief Superintendent! I was thinking of my husband's. He was a major general, you know. As an officer he had a service revolver but I am speaking of a rather special pistol which was given him by a maharajah. The butt was inlaid with silver and it carried an inscription. "Given in friendship to Major General George Burnett-Price, C.B.E., M.C., September 1947." George was very proud of it.'

'Where is it now?' Wycliffe's manner was such that he could have been a doctor enquiring about a patient's symptoms rather than a policeman conducting a case.

She patted her hair in a vain attempt to control the wispy escapes. 'I don't know: it's gone.'

'When did you last see it?'

She looked at him, frowning. 'Months ago, it could be a year. I'd forgotten all about it.'

'What reminded you?'

'Why, the Lemarques, what else? Both of them were shot were they not?' Her voice faltered and suddenly all trace of her rather coy silliness vanished, leaving her a sad and very worried old woman. She smoothed her skirt then clasped her bony misshapen hands in her lap. 'It was late last night; I was sitting here brooding on the Lemarques when it occurred to me that if they had been shot . . .' She hesitated and stopped speaking as though she wished to rephrase what she was about to say; then

157

she went on: 'I thought I ought to see if George's pistol was in its proper place, in the cupboard where I kept it.'

'Why connect your husband's pistol with what happened to Jane and Alain Lemarque?'

She was silent for a time. Somewhere in the house somebody was using a vacuum cleaner while outside the window gulls were screeching. When she spoke her manner was petulant.

'Do you think this is Chicago, Chief Superintendent? How many guns would you expect to find in Mulfra?' Whatever the shortcomings of her memory, she was shrewd.

'Go on.'

'Well, I looked for the gun and it wasn't there.'

Wycliffe said: 'Just now you spoke of your husband's service revolver, but you called the gun given him by the maharajah, a pistol – do you know the difference between a pistol and a revolver?'

She was contemptuous. 'I wasn't married to an army officer for nearly fifty years without learning something about firearms. In fact, when we were in India I did a certain amount of target shooting myself.'

'Show me where the gun was kept.'

She went to one of the cupboards below the glass-fronted display cases and brought out a sandalwood box. He saw a look of astonishment on her old face as she lifted the box but she said nothing. She placed it on a low table and raised the lid.

Inside were gun-cleaning materials and a chamois leather pouch in the shape of a holster. The butt of an automatic pistol, inlaid with silver, protruded from the pouch.

The old lady looked at the contents of the box in bewilderment, then at him. 'I don't understand! It wasn't there last night.' She repeated with emphasis: 'It really was not there!'

She put out her hand to pick up the pistol.

'Don't touch it!' He went on: 'So you are quite sure the gun was not in its place last night?'

She nodded. 'I wish to God I wasn't.'

'Can you tell me what sort of gun this is?'

She went back to her chair and sat down, obviously distressed. In a tired voice she said: 'It's a Walther P-38. German – that was the one thing which disappointed George. Of course they are wonderful pistols but he hadn't got over the war . . . '

Wycliffe murmured: 'Jane Lemarque was killed with a .38 automatic, almost certainly a Walther.'

She said nothing but he saw her hands tighten on the arms of her chair.

He spoke gently: 'I shall have to take this away with me for tests – box and all. Were there any cartridges?'

She made a feeble gesture with her hand. 'That little cardboard box in with the gun: there were a few single cartridges in that. I don't know how many . . . or how many are left.' She went on as though speaking to herself: 'To think that someone took the pistol . . . and put it back. They must have put it back in the night . . . they must have!'

'Who knew that you had this gun?'

'Who knew? Why, everybody must have known about it when it was presented to George – all the family, I mean.'

'But that was thirty-seven years ago. Most of the people in this house now were either very young or they had not been born.'

This brought her up short. 'I hadn't thought of that. One forgets how time passes . . . '

'When did you come to Mynhager to live?'

'Three years ago; after poor George died. Before that we lived in Dorset.'

'Did you speak to anyone about the gun then or have you mentioned it since?'

She shook her head. 'I don't think so. I can't remember.' She was becoming agitated. 'I just don't know!'

He was sorry for her. 'I know this is very distressing for you but I want you to say nothing about it to anyone for the time being. Will you agree to that?'

'If you say so.'

'I'll give you a receipt for the box and its contents.' He wrote out a receipt and handed it to her. 'Just one question: Who, in your opinion, could have come into your room during the night or this morning to put the gun back?'

She looked at him, frowning. 'Anyone! Anyone at all. I close my bedroom door at night so I wouldn't have heard anyone in this room.'

'And this morning?'

'This morning?' She looked troubled and a certain vagueness returned to her manner. He mustn't push her too far.

But she went on: 'This morning I got up at seven as I usually do and my breakfast was brought to me here at eight-thirty. I was here until just before you arrived.'

He left, carrying the sandalwood box in a Marks and Spencer bag she had given him. In the hall he encountered Bateman who was obviously intrigued by the bag but did not refer to it.

'Did you speak to my father-in-law?'

'No. I'm afraid that wasn't possible; I spent some time with Mrs Burnett-Price.'

A suave smile.

Bateman saw him off.

His thoughts were sombre. Two guns, one a revolver belonging to Lemarque, the other, an automatic, belonging to Stella Burnett-Price but accessible to the whole household at Mynhager.

It now seemed that the Lemarques had both been murdered by the same hand and that he was in possession of the weapon. Jane Lemarque had died at some time after four-thirty on Christmas Eve, her husband probably earlier, at about three o'clock.

Wycliffe's thoughts went back to that day. In the

morning he had been at the Lemarques' cottage with Virginia; he had lunched with the family at Mynhager and afterwards, feeling drowsy from too much drink, he had dozed in an armchair in the drawing-room until Curtis arrived. He recalled that he had joined Curtis in the dining-room at half-past three, by which time Lemarque must have been already dead . . .

Had he seen any of the others after lunch? Caroline and Ernest in the kitchen; she was making a brandy trifle and he was dipping his fingers in the cream . . . Then he and Curtis had gone to see Marsden. He was back at Mynhager in good time for dinner at seven . . . He had gone to his room and by that time Jane Lemarque was almost certainly dead.

Was it possible that he had sat at table that evening with a double murderer?

He was walking back along the track to the village; the Mini was still parked outside Marsden's cottage but now the back was packed, almost to the roof, with cardboard boxes and bulging polythene bags. As he reached the cottage the young woman he had seen before came out of the front door carrying yet another bag. She looked at him with a hint of aggression. A handsome blonde, in peevish mood.

'Is Mr Marsden at home?'

'No.'

'I am Chief Superintendent Wycliffe.'

'I know. If you want him you'll find him at The Tributers.' She bundled her latest bag in on top of the rest and slammed the car door. As she turned away she seemed surprised to find him still standing there.

'Perhaps you will give me a few minutes of your time.'

She was about to refuse but thought better of it. 'All right, but you'd better come inside.'

In the living-room he was not asked to sit down. The fire in the grate had gone out and Marsden's cat was sleeping in the fender. The table was littered with an even greater accumulation of dirty dishes and empty tins. The girl stood by the table, hands thrust deep into the pockets of her bush jacket, waiting.

'You are Miss . . .'

'Call me Emma.'

He realized that this was not a concession, rather a refusal to tell him her surname. 'Your name, please?'

'Emma Gregory.'

'You've lived here for how long?'

'Nearly a year.'

'And now you are moving out.'

'As you see.' Her jaw set in a hard line.

'You know that Mr and Mrs Lemarque are both dead?'

'I knew about Mrs Lemarque; he told me about the husband this morning.'

'You mean that Mr Marsden told you?'

'Yes.'

'Since you have lived here have either of the Lemarques called on Mr Marsden?'

'I work in St Ives; I've no idea what happens when I'm away, but I've never seen her here.'

'What about Mr Lemarque?'

'He's only been out of jail a few weeks but in that time he's called twice in the evenings – that is to say when I've been here.'

'Did he stay long?'

An impatient movement. 'I wasn't watching the clock. About an hour each time, I suppose. They went into the studio to talk, presumably because they didn't want me to hear what was said.'

'Perhaps they were discussing pictures.'

'Perhaps.'

'Did they seem friendly to each other?'

'Not especially.'

'What does that mean?'

'That they didn't seem particularly friendly.'

Wycliffe snapped: 'Don't play games, Miss Gregory! In what way did they seem unfriendly?'

162

She had flushed at his change of tone. She was not as hard as she pretended. 'Well, Hugh didn't seem pleased to see him and when they were in the studio I heard Hugh's voice raised several times. Of course it doesn't take much to make him shout.'

'On Lemarque's first visit did Marsden seem surprised to see him?'

'That wasn't my impression.' She glanced at her watch. 'If there's nothing more I've got a lot to do.'

'I won't keep you but I would like your address in case we need to get in touch.'

She hesitated, realized that it was pointless to refuse and said: 'Emma Gregory, 14, Seaview Road, Penzance. But I hope you won't want me, my parents have had more than enough to put up with as it is.'

He continued on his way back to the village. Clouds which had been building over the hills were spreading seawards, obscuring the sun, and as he reached the van the first drops of rain began to fall. It was one o'clock and Kersey was waiting.

Wycliffe put his carrier bag on the table.

'Been shopping, sir?'

'I want this properly packed and sent by special messenger for ballistic tests.'

Kersey was made to feel that his humour was ill-timed but he wasn't easily repressed. 'Is one allowed to enquire where it came from?'

Wycliffe brought him up to date then he put through a call to a friend in Ballistics asking for most urgent treatment.

'One more thing before we eat.' Once more Wycliffe produced his envelope with the newscutting. 'I want someone to go through the Incident Records for anything of note occurring in this area on the 15th and 16th of April 1979.'

'I'll see to it, sir.'

They walked across to The Tributers with the rain gathering purpose, and went up to their rooms to wash.

'See you in the bar later.'

Wycliffe was the first down; he had to pass the open door of the kitchen to reach the bar. Phyllis was in the kitchen, wearing a white apron, cutting up meat on a floury board. There were several little heaps on the board.

'Do you like pasties – real Cornish pasties, I mean?'

'What? Yes, I think so . . .'

She laughed. 'Bless the man! He's miles away. Pasties – that's what you'll get this evening unless you say different now.'

'Yes, pasties – very nice.'

In the bar less than half the tables were occupied but Marsden was there reading a newspaper, a glass of ale, an empty soup bowl and a spread of crumbs in front of him. He acknowledged Wycliffe with a lift of the hand.

Lorna was behind the bar, archly familiar: 'So what can we do for you today?'

'A half of home-brew.'

'Nothing to eat?'

'I'll wait for Mr Kersey.'

He took his drink to a table by the window. It was raining hard now, vertical silvery cords blotted out the view and the gloom inside made it difficult to see across the bar. Lorna switched on the lights. 'Let the dog see the rabbit.'

Kersey arrived and they ordered bowls of soup and bread rolls with garlic butter.

Kersey spoke in a low voice: 'I had a bit of news this morning about our friend. My mate called. He's station officer now. He remembered the case but he's been digging around for details. Of course it was four years ago.'

Wycliffe was staring across at the painter who seemed absorbed in his newspaper. Kersey wasn't sure whether to go on or not. In the end he said: 'He can't hear us.'

Wycliffe seemed indifferent.

'Marsden was charged with selling a painting of his

own, executed in the style of and purporting to be the work of another – in English, flogging a fake. They could have brought half-a-dozen similar charges but the one they chose referred to an alleged Gauguin. He sold it through a go-between to a seemingly reputable dealer. The case didn't hold up in court because the jury couldn't make up their minds at what stage the picture was provided with its forged documentation or who added a spidery little "P Gauguin" in one corner of the picture.'

Kersey waited but Wycliffe went on with his meal.

'Don't you want to know the name of this reputable dealer?'

Wycliffe muttered something.

'Lemarque Galleries Limited; a subsidiary of Lemarque Holdings.'

Wycliffe emptied his soup bowl and patted his lips with a paper napkin. 'You may be right. Lemarque's organization may have had dealings on the shady side of the street and it's possible that Marsden worked for him. The fact that the two of them have been in contact since Lemarque came out of jail seems to support the idea and we should know more when we get a report on the Lemarque/Bateman partnership. But we are looking for a motive for the murder of Lemarque and his wife by someone who had access to the pistol kept in Stella Burnett-Price's room. That limits the range of motives as it limits the number of suspects.'

'But it leaves Bateman in with a chance.'

Wycliffe got to his feet. 'If you've finished your meal let's go.'

Kersey said: 'What meal?'

CHAPTER TEN

As they left Marsden once more raised his hand in casual salutation.

Wycliffe was worried – afraid, yet he could think of no particular reason for fear. The killer had done his work (her work?) so all that remained for him to do was to 'identify and apprehend' as they used to say in the days when quite ordinary people spoke English. And if he was right about the pistol he had only to look among that small circle which formed the household at Mynhager. The process would be painful but the outcome certain.

They crossed the square to the van in drenching rain which was coming down faster than the drains could carry it away. As they were hanging up their waterproofs Kersey said: 'Something wrong?'

'The girl. I'd feel happier if we could get her away from Mynhager.'

Wycliffe went into the cubicle he had adopted as his temporary office and slid himself on to the bench between table and wall.

'How did you get on with Rosemergy Minerals?'

Kersey stood in the doorway. 'I've got an appointment in Penzance at 2.30 with a chap called Trewhella, their estate manager.' He glanced at his watch. 'I'd better get started.'

Wycliffe was left to brood on his in-tray. Away from headquarters he missed the guiding hand and steely resolve of his personal assistant, Diane. Diane, the immaculate, would never have permitted such an accumulation. The mound consisted of reports and memoranda, each one with an attached tag on which he was expected to indicate how the item should be dealt with.

He picked up the first document, glanced through it, and slipped it to the bottom of the pile; the next he initialled for filing, and the next. The fourth item was the little page-depleted notebook which he had found under Francine's bed and stopped her from taking away. Why? Now his action seemed insensitive and officious. But there had been something odd about the way she had darted back into the room at the last moment, something self-consciously deceitful in her manner which seemed out of character. At the same time he was prepared to believe that retrieving the notebook had been her main purpose in going upstairs.

He turned over a few pages. Francine's writing had character, a mature hand, bold and decisive. But her style was cryptic. He was reminded of his rough notebook at school where barely comprehensible statements were interspersed with doodles and unflattering sketches of the teacher. No sketches here.

'Blue-eyed people homozygous for recessive but more to it than that: Modifiers. Possible for blue-eyed parents to have brown-eyed child but only a 1:50 chance.' The figures were ringed.

'Dark hair dominant to blond but dark-haired parents can have redheads or auburn-haired offspring.'

There was a page on blood grouping on the ABO system with two heavily underlined sentences: 'Not possible for parents both lacking agglutinogen B to have a child of group B or AB.' And: 'For a mother of group A to have a child AB the father would have to be group B or AB.'

The last page was blank except for the query: 'Body form?'

The telephone rang. 'Records for you, sir.'

A list of incidents in the area on 15/16 April 1979, covering the night of the professional men's dinner in

Penzance. The clerk gabbled through them. A routine lot: a couple of break-ins; a spate of minor R.T.A.s; vandalism on the promenade at Penzance, youths tearing up flower beds . . . The only major incident, a hit-and-run with a young girl killed and her body left in the ditch. This, at some time after midnight in, of all places, a country lane between Badger's Cross and New Mill.

'Was the driver traced?'

'No, sir. The file remains open. There was strong suspicion but insufficient evidence.'

Wycliffe vaguely recalled the case through reports. 'Send the file on to me here.'

He spread an Ordnance map on his table and identified the lane in which the girl had been killed then he called in D.C. Curnow. 'I believe you come from these parts?'

'Born and brought up in Penzance, sir.'

'You know this lane?'

'Very well. It runs past the site of the iron-age village at Chysauster.'

'You wouldn't go that way if you were driving from Penzance here, I imagine?'

'Certainly I wouldn't, sir. You can see it puts a good distance on the trip and the road is poor – no more than a country lane.'

'Is it much used?'

'There's a fair amount of traffic in the summer with visitors to the site but otherwise, next to nothing.'

Well, he would give the file an airing. Curnow returned to his cubby-hole and a minute or two later there was another telephone call. Pigeons returning to roost, bread which had been cast upon the waters . . . This time, Sergeant Fox with a preliminary report on the recovered van:

'I've been over the vehicle with Alan Taylor from Forensic. Of course, there's all the detailed work still to be done but we've got identifiable prints. In the driving compartment Lemarque's dabs are all over the place;

168

with two or three of hers in the passenger seat area. No strangers in the front of the van. The same applies to the exterior bodywork, but in the load compartment, apart from Lemarque's we found three sets all from male subjects; two belonging to the same man and fairly old, the third recent and fresh.

'We've collected dust and other detritus samples and Taylor is taking them back for examination.'

'Any sign of blood or other body tissue?'

'None, sir. Of course the door on the driver's side was not recovered but Taylor thinks it virtually impossible that the man could have shot himself while in the driving seat, causing the wound of exit described, without contamination of the interior.'

So Lemarque had not shot himself in the act of driving over the cliff; neither had he shot himself nor been shot in the van. Was it conceivable that he had pushed his van over, then shot himself as he jumped? Fantasy! Lemarque had been murdered as his wife had been murdered.

He drew geometrical designs on his scratch pad but his thoughts were far from forming any rational sequence. He sometimes said that he was incapable of real thought because his mind was preoccupied with recollected pictures, with snatches of conversation, and incidents of dubious relevance, which presented themselves with compelling clarity but in random sequence. He would play with his recollections, fitting them together, discarding and rearranging, until he made a credible pattern. 'Like a child playing with bricks,' he told himself. Did they still play with bricks? Or with computer graphics?

Francine with the shepherds' posies . . . 'and purple for Death'.

The Lemarque's living-room where the two of them played out their mysterious charade for his benefit and for Virginia's. Why had they suppressed the note which Francine said she had written?

169

Jane Lemarque wedged between dressing table and bed with half her face blown away.

Alain Lemarque, his little simian body distended, lying on the quay in a puddle of seawater which had drained from his clothing.

'She's never been the same since Francine was born . . .'

'Why does she do it – go off like that?' . . . 'To punish me.'

'She's only trying to make an impression on her mother . . . Lemarque spent years trying to do the same thing and look where it landed him . . .'

'She let him go to bed with her.'

'Mother has to tell everything.'

And mother had told Evadne Penrose: ' . . . he must have taken the gun!'

Of another gun Aunt Stella had said: 'It wasn't there last night . . . They must have put it back . . .'

So many fragments of memory. They crowded in, taking possession of his mind and seeming to jockey for position. Now there was this damned notebook.

'Not possible for parents both lacking agglutinogen B . . .'

He brought his fist down on the table and probably woke D.S. Shaw in the next cubicle. He picked up the telephone. 'Try to get Dr Franks on the line.'

For once Franks was in his room at the hospital. 'Not another body for me, Charles?'

'I suppose you did blood grouping tests on the Lemarques?'

'As a matter of routine. I don't put the results in my preliminary report unless they seem relevant. If you hold on I'll look them up.'

Franks didn't keep him long. 'Jane Lemarque was Group A Rhesus positive, and her husband, also Rhesus positive, was Group O.'

'So they could not have had an AB child?'

'You know the answer to that as well as I do, Charles.'

So Francine was not Alain Lemarque's daughter. Not

difficult to believe, but hardly a motive for double murder, though it might explain a good deal about Francine.

Four-thirty, and already it was dark. The lights were on in the van and he pulled down the blind. Deprived of his pipe, he played with matches from a box Kersey had left behind. By slotting the ends with his penknife he contrived a creature which suggested a cross between a donkey and a kangaroo and when Kersey arrived back from his appointment in Penzance he found his chief putting the finishing touches to this chimera.

'Make another and we could race 'em.'

Kersey inserted himself into the bench seat and Wycliffe brought him up to date but he was unimpressed.

'So the girl was conceived on the wrong side of the duvet. Who was her real father? One of the Mynhager lot? If so, sexual limitations being what they are, there aren't many candidates. There's Ernest, Bateman, and the old man. But really, sir, who is likely to worry unduly about it after nearly seventeen years?'

Wycliffe said: 'The girl, perhaps.' But he agreed with Kersey. 'Anyway, how did you get on in Penzance?'

'Tim Trewhella, their estate manager, is a decent chap. He was helpful once he'd grasped the situation. It seems Lemarque approached him about a month ago with a scheme for leasing and developing the Mennear Bal site. He'd worked it out, presumably during his long idle hours in the nick. The idea was to clear the site to within 200 metres of the cliff and lay it out for chalets and touring caravans with a swimming pool, restaurant, shop and the rest.

'Trewhella asked about capital and Lemarque said he had one backer for £50,000 and, once the scheme was launched, he had no doubt he could raise the rest.'

'Was the backer's name mentioned?'

'Apparently not.'

'What about planning?'

'Lemarque reckoned that the authorities would play

171

along because the scheme would reclaim an industrial wasteland in an area of great natural beauty.'

Wycliffe, a conservationist, said: 'Of the two, I'd prefer the mine dumps. Sounds like a pipe dream to me.'

'Me too. Trewhella said businessmen are liable to these flights of fancy and that reality only moves in with the accountants.'

Wycliffe adjusted the hind-legs of his creature so that it stood properly. 'You think it likely that Bateman committed himself to put £50,000 into that?'

'Perhaps Lemarque was in a position to squeeze; in which case we have a man with a motive.'

'For a double murder? Anyway we shan't get much further along those lines until we hear from John Scales what he's been able to find out about the Lemarque/ Bateman partnership.' He picked up the telephone and asked to be put through to D.C.I. Scales at police headquarters.

'Is that you, John? . . . About the Lemarque/Bateman partnership . . . It's the information I want, John, not bits of paper to stick in a file . . .'

Kersey thought: Temper! He's missing his pipe.

Wycliffe wedged the phone against his neck while he went through the clumsy ritual of putting on his spectacles, then he began to scribble notes. It was five minutes before he put down the phone and turned back to Kersey.

'Lemarque was a bigger rogue than we've taken him for. The Bishops gave the impression that he was a victim of circumstance but according to this he was operating several profitable rackets in the art trade: fencing choice items of stolen property, arranging illicit export deals, and handling fakes . . . He had a high powered organization with two or three recognized experts on his pay-roll. The Met, using a softly-softly approach, were building up a nice dossier when there was a leak, somebody pressed the self-destruct button

172

and the organization just melted away. At the finish the Met boys were left with red faces and Lemarque on a comparatively minor charge.'

'What about Bateman?'

'According to this he was responsible for the antiques side of the business – a separate company which seems to have been more or less above board. Bateman's main source of embarrassment came from an alleged statement by Lemarque, quoted in a coat-trailing Sunday paper, to the effect that if he went to jail he could take Bateman with him. There was a libel action against the paper, settled out of court, but there were awkward questions and for a time it looked bleak for Bateman politically, then it all blew over.'

'So where do we go from here?'

'We talk to Marsden. If he can't do anything else he may be able to throw a bit more light on the Bateman/Lemarque set-up.'

'Now?'

'Why not?'

Outside, the rain had stopped and the air was clear and fresh. 'We'll walk.'

As they turned down the track by the pub they could hear the slow ripping sound of waves breaking along the shoreline. There was a light in Marsden's cottage and the music this time was neither jazz nor Bach but Tchaikovsky's *1812*, blasting hell out of the French and everyone else within range.

They had to bang on the door before Marsden heard them above the racket but their reception was not unfriendly. 'I suppose it's no use telling you I'm busy? You'd better come in.'

He switched off the record player and the instant silence assaulted the ears. With a certain reverence he slid the record back into its sleeve. 'Poor Peter Ilyich died from drinking water; a warning to us all.'

To Wycliffe's surprise the table had been cleared of dirty dishes and was now covered by a chenille cloth; the

173

floor, too, looked reasonably free of debris. The painter read his thoughts: 'Yes, well, when you don't have a dog you have to do your own barking.'

A fire burned in the grate and Percy lay at full stretch on the hearth-rug.

Marsden looked at Kersey: 'What's this then, a new stooge?'

'Detective Inspector Kersey.'

Kersey said: 'We've met before.'

Marsden looked him over. 'The occasion escapes me.'

'Paddington Green nick, 1980.'

'I was acquitted.'

Wycliffe lifted a bundle of newspapers off a chair and sat down. 'All the same, whether you signed them or not, whether you provided the authentication or not, you painted fakes for Lemarque Galleries.'

Marsden pushed a low stool in Kersey's direction and sat in his own armchair. 'Correction on two counts: I did not paint fakes; I painted pictures "in the style of" and I did not deal with Lemarque Galleries but, believe it or not, with The Stylov Gallery – Stylov – get it? You need to be six years old to really appreciate the subtlety of these guys. They had a shop in Kensington where they sold pictures in the style of almost any painter you fancied. Nothing illegal about it; all open and above board except for the mark-up they put on a poor bastard's blood and sweat. A couple of us did the grind and they collected.

'Say you wanted a picture in the style of that celebrated French Impressionist, Le Merde; if they hadn't got one in the racks, they would provide me with a suitable stretcher, I would refresh my memory of the gentleman's palette, style and technique and get cracking.

'It worked well enough until Lemarque Galleries bought out Stylov as a front to get hold of suitable canvases for "upgrading".' A throaty chuckle.

'And you expect us to believe that you didn't know what was going on?'

174

'All that matters to me is that the jury believed it.'

'Or had their doubts.'

'As you say, but their doubts were good enough for me. By the way, that was a damn fine Gauguin. The old rogue would have liked it and it would have taken me in if I hadn't painted it.'

Wycliffe said: 'But not, apparently, the experts.'

Marsden was contemptuous. 'Experts my arse! The clowns slipped up on the paperwork.'

Kersey lit a cigarette and threw the dead match in the direction of the fireplace. 'How come you end up down here within spitting distance of Lemarque and his former partner?'

Marsden picked up Kersey's match and put it in the fire. 'A gesture on the part of the old firm when the balloon was about to go up.'

'To encourage you to keep your mouth shut.'

'A reward for services rendered to art.'

'Not as a suitable base to start a spot of blackmail?'

Marsden coughed bronchially and spat in the fire. 'You'll find that horse won't run. Not my line.'

The room was utterly silent. Perhaps that was why Marsden felt the need from time to time to drench himself in sound. He settled back in his chair; a cigarette plaeed centrally between his lips seemed in imminent danger of setting his moustache alight.

Wycliffe said: 'These visits you've been receiving from Lemarque since he came out of prison: what was he after?'

Marsden looked mildly put out. 'Emma's been talking. Why are women so spiteful? Lemarque wanted to revive the Stylov caper; he's been scratching about looking for a new launch pad. He'd given himself twelve months. "In a year, one way or another, I'll be back up there – or I'll shoot myself." That sort of talk. I told him he'd have to manage without me. I've gone soft since I've been down here and I've got used to crowing on my own dung heap. What's more I've come to prefer genuine Marsdens to Stylov versions of museum fodder.'

'You told me that you had no contact with Lemarque.'

'A tiny fib in an ocean of truth.'

'In your position you can't afford such luxuries.'

Wycliffe tried another approach. 'Lemarque is supposed to have said that he could have taken Bateman to jail with him. What did you make of that?'

'A shot across the bows.'

'You mean he could have done it?'

A moment for consideration: 'I doubt it, but the threat would have made Bateman think twice about joining the hounds.'

'In your opinion was Bateman involved in fraud?'

Marsden chuckled. 'My God! What a question! Let's say that in copper's terms he was probably in the clear.'

Some clarification; no enlightenment. They walked back to The Tributers and to Phyllis's pasties which spanned ten-inch dinner plates.

Afterwards Wycliffe said, 'Well, we're as fully briefed as we are ever likely to be. By the morning we should have official confirmation that it was the old lady's pistol which killed Jane Lemarque and that gives us the necessary cover if anyone wants to get legalistic.'

'So?'

'So tomorrow we move in. Formal interviews and statements from every member of the household. I want you to do it with whatever assistance you need. Pick your own men. I shall hold a watching brief.'

'I'll fix it from the duty roster.' Kersey hesitated. 'I take it you want this done by the book – uniformed men outside?'

'By the book.'

Wycliffe walked across to the Incident Van where D.C. Curnow was duty officer until shut-down at ten o'clock.

Curnow, an earnest young man, put down an improving book. 'This arrived by messenger, sir.'

The file on the hit-and-run, a formidable bundle.

Wycliffe skimmed through it. A nineteen-year-old

176

girl was walking home after visiting a friend. Less than a mile separated their two houses. She was in one of the widest sections of the lane when, according to the pathologist, she was hit from behind by a vehicle travelling at a fair speed. In the off-season the lane was little used except by a few people who lived along it, and even during the day traffic was minimal.

Again, according to the pathologist, after the accident the girl's body had been dragged off the road into the ditch. The scene of the incident, worked over by experts, yielded nothing, mainly because of torrential rain later that night. The inquiry had been thorough: over 200 people questioned; publicans within a range of fifteen miles interviewed, and garage owners quizzed about damaged vehicles. Suspicion rested on a local character who at the time was under a ban for a drunken driving offence. But there was no real evidence and his alibi, though it offended police nostrils, could not be broken. The only possible material clue was a few fragments of glass recovered from the scene. According to the experts they were not from the fittings of any vehicle and probably had nothing to do with the incident.

Wycliffe put the documents back in the file. Almost certainly an irrelevance. But why had Lemarque kept that press cutting?

Anyway, tomorrow they would move into Mynhager with all the ammunition they could hope to have in order to ask the right questions and be able to judge the answers. But tonight?

He was uneasy.

Curnow was ready to shut up shop for the night. With the rest of the headquarters team he was lodging in Penzance. Wycliffe signed the book and by the time he had reached the door of The Tributers the church clock was striking ten and the lights had gone out in the caravan.

He spent an hour with Kersey, working out the strategy for the morning.

*

Sleep would not come; he resigned himself and tried to resolve the confusion of his thoughts with one more review of the facts and their interpretation.

The Lemarques had been murdered and the sequence of events seemed clear. The killer made an appointment to meet Lemarque at the site of his proposed tourist park, ostensibly to discuss plans; in fact, to kill him. Lemarque was shot and his body pushed over the cliff. Later the van was driven erratically along the track and pushed over, to convey the impression of a suicidal act.

The van disposed of, the killer went to the cottage and in what must have been a horrifying scene, shot Jane Lemarque. He then left the cottage and Wycliffe believed that he had seen the light of the man's hand torch from the other side of the valley.

The crux of the problem was motive. Jane Lemarque was killed because she might have been able to point to her husband's killer; more than that, the strategy of the crime was to suggest that Lemarque had committed suicide after killing his wife. But why was Lemarque killed?

There was no evidence that Bateman was being blackmailed for his part in the Lemarque frauds; in fact there was no indication that he had been criminally involved. The question of Francine's parentage provided no grounds for murder. There is no longer any blackmail in bastardy.

Wycliffe sat up in bed and pounded his pillow. The room was cold and the light from the street lamp coming through the curtains had a frosty brightness. Enough light to see the time by his travelling clock: a quarter past one. His thoughts had been going round in circles for two hours and he had indigestion. He had eaten Phyllis's pasty too greedily. He got out of bed, padded across to the washbasin, and drank half-a-glass of water from his tooth mug.

Back in bed, chilled, he still could not settle down. The pistol, the Walther P.38 with its inscribed silver plate, seemed to pin the crime down to Mynhager. Would he be in the absurd position of knowing the criminal without having discovered the motive? And what had happened to Lemarque's revolver?

Lemarque. From the day of his release he had set about promoting the new enterprises he had dreamed up in jail. 'In a year, one way or another, I'll be back up there, or I'll shoot myself!' All his activity seemed to be directed to this single end: his contacts with Rosemergy Minerals, with Bateman, with Marsden, his trips in the van and his surreptitious telephone calls sometimes cut short by the arrival of Francine.

Those telephone calls. What was it Francine had overheard him say? Something about five years ago and being in the same boat . . . 'Five years ago we were all three in the same boat, or should I say car? Not any more!' Something like that anyway.

Suddenly the words acquired a new and threatening significance. It was five years since the girl's death in a hit-and-run. 'All in the same boat, or should I say car?'

Wycliffe turned over violently, sweeping the bedclothes along with him. Was it possible . . . ?

CHAPTER ELEVEN

A clear and almost windless morning. Hoar-frost on the slopes.

'Just coffee and toast for me, Phyllis.'

'And me.'

A buttery laugh. 'Indigestion, I'll be bound! Didn't I say you had to work or walk down a pasty? Instead you spend your time sitting around, the pair of you. What you need after a pasty, apart from a bit of exercise, is a drink of tea – about an hour after, for preference, and with a bit of sugar in it. I don't hold with sugar in tea as a rule but after a pasty 'tis the best thing if you don't want to be going for the bicarbonate later.'

When they were alone Kersey said: 'Did I hear you go downstairs some time in the early morning?'

'I went for a drive.'

'Good God! Are you going to tell me about it?'

'Later, in the van.'

They were at the van well before nine but just in time to take a call from Forbes, the ballistics expert. Forbes was one of those fortunate people who are paid for work which they find totally absorbing. He functioned in a sound-proof basement and the succession of day and night meant as much to him as to a mole.

'I've only done the preliminary work on this one, Charles, but I can tell you that the bullet and cartridge case found at the scene of the crime were from the Walther P.38 you sent me yesterday. The rifling and striation marks on the bullet, and the extraction marks and head scratches on the case correspond precisely with those on the test-fired specimens. No doubt at all.

Incidentally the Walther wasn't properly cleaned after firing and it hadn't been looked after before that. It's had very little use – probably fired less than half-a-dozen rounds since it was new in the mid-forties. The mechanism is stiff and the clown who used it was lucky it didn't jam.' Forbes felt about firearms as others feel about pets and children. 'Criminal to neglect such a nice mechanism!'

Wycliffe spent a few minutes looking over the newspapers. Ella Bunt's story had been taken up by the rest of Fleet Street to be re-run with variations and given extra punch by the discovery of Lemarque's body. The Cornish murders were news.

Kersey said: 'I'm more interested in your night driving. What made you go off in the small hours?'

Wycliffe explained.

Then the moment he had been waiting for and dreading. The evidence of the pistol made it certain that the killer of Jane Lemarque and, by extension, of her husband, was a member of the household at Mynhager.

He turned to Kersey. 'Are we ready?'

'All lined up, sir.'

Wycliffe, Kersey, D.S. Shaw, and a female clerk-typist, a blonde with a pretty little snub nose and a portable typewriter, went in Wycliffe's car. Two uniformed men followed in a Panda. At shortly after eleven o'clock they set out. Two cars one behind the other on a deserted track make a procession and so it must have seemed when they arrived in the courtyard at Mynhager. Even against the background of a glittering sea the house looked grim. Wycliffe had discovered that Mynhager could be translated from the Cornish as 'edge parlous'. It was apt; it had a sinister Arthurian ring.

One of the uniformed men remained in the courtyard; the other took up his post on the terrace. Anyone wishing to enter or leave the house would have to account for themselves. Kersey was aware of Wycliffe's intense distaste for what had to be done, and sympathized.

181

Ernest answered their ring. 'Ah, Charles! I suppose this is an official visit? You'd better come in.'

In the dim, cave-like hall the silence was punctuated by the majestic ticking of the grandfather clock. Wycliffe introduced his men. 'Inspector Kersey and Sergeant Shaw will be conducting the interviews . . . It would be helpful if they could have a room where they can be private and undisturbed.'

'The dining-room, perhaps . . .'

It would have been obvious to Ernest that something of the sort was bound to happen, he must have been expecting it. He escorted them to the dining-room. The heavy velvet curtains were almost meeting across the window allowing only a strip of light to enter. But it was warm; there were two of the Albert Hall type radiators.

'I hope this will suit you.'

Kersey said that it would, very well.

Ernest was pale and he looked as though he had lost a lot of sleep. His manner was dry, distant, and correct. They could hardly expect anything else.

Sergeant Shaw settled himself with his notebook and papers at one end of the long table. Unlike some of his colleagues, Shaw was always formally dressed and he might have been taken for the family solicitor on a business visit. The typist found a small table for her machine near the window.

Kersey said: 'I wonder if you can tell me, sir, whether any members of the household are out at the moment?'

Ernest went to the window and drew back the curtains so that light off the sea flooded into the room to combat its drabness. He said: 'I don't keep a register of comings and goings, Mr Kersey, but we are all here as far as I know.'

Shaw made an entry on one of his sheets of paper.

Kersey said: 'Thank you, sir. Could we start with Miss Bishop?'

Ernest looked surprised. Perhaps he had expected to head the list.

To Wycliffe the proceedings, although familiar enough in other settings, seemed unreal. Virginia arrived looking apprehensive. She took the seat Kersey offered, looking up at Wycliffe as though in some hope that he might be taking over, but he joined Ernest in the hall.

'I would like to talk to your father if that is convenient.'

'I'll take you to him.'

Up the stairs and along the corridor, past the room where he had slept as a guest. Joseph's room was at the end of the passage. Ernest tapped on the door and opened it.

'A visitor for you, father.'

The old man was sitting by the window, a book on his lap. He dropped a half-smoked cheroot in the ashtray and got up. 'Ah, Wycliffe! Come in, my dear fellow, sit down . . .'

'Charles is here officially, father.'

'So? What difference does that make? He can still sit down, I suppose?'

'I'll leave you with father, Charles.'

As the door closed the old man said: 'He's never learned to be objective; always tripping over his own emotional bootlaces. So you're getting down to business and you've come to tell me about it.'

It was the first time Wycliffe had been in Joseph's room. The bow window opened up a tremendous panoramic sweep and the old man made an expansive gesture. 'This window faces due west, nothing between me and White Bay Newfoundland except, and thank God for it, the Gulf Stream.'

Wycliffe stayed on course: 'I had confirmation this morning that Jane Lemarque was shot with the pistol presented to your late brother-in-law Major General Burnett-Price. It seems likely that Alain Lemarque was shot with the same weapon but because of the circumstances we have no proof.'

Joseph picked up his cheroot which had gone out and threw it away. 'Go on.'

'Your sister looked for the pistol on Tueday night and she was distressed to find that it was not in its usual place. Yesterday, Wednesday, she called me in to tell me it was missing but when she showed me where it was usually kept, there it was.'

The old man stroked his moustache with the back of his hand. 'And your boffins were able to show that the gun had been recently fired?'

'More than that, they are able to prove that the bullet and cartridge case recovered at the scene of the crime came from that pistol.'

It was impossible to say how much of this was already known to him or guessed at but the old man had not batted an eyelid. 'So you concluded that someone in this house was responsible, certainly for the first crime.'

'I concluded that I had grounds for doing what is now being done.'

A shrewd glance. 'Of course! I wouldn't quarrel with that. You think you've established the means, that leaves opportunity and motive. I'm afraid I can't help you with either. I spent the whole of Christmas Eve afternoon here, conserving my energy for the festivities. I don't think I saw anyone – yes I did! At about four Ernest brought me my tea and biscuits; one of the women usually brings it but I gathered they were otherwise engaged.'

Wycliffe looked about him. It was obvious that the room and the man had grown together to such a point that separation would destroy them both. The paintings, the photographs, the books and the furniture were as much part of him as his memories, and together they constituted his life. Did he see them as threatened? If so, how far would he go in their defence?

'My wife, Ursula.'

Wycliffe happened at that moment to be looking at the only portrait in the room, a head-and-shoulders painting of a very beautiful young woman. Her light-auburn hair was coiled on top of her head; her attention

184

seemed to be directed at something far away and one had the rather absurd impression that the painter had taken her unawares.

'She was nineteen when that was done. She had an identical twin sister, Gerald's mother. We are an inbred family.' The old man chuckled. 'Perhaps in danger of becoming incestuous.'

It was a fine performance. He was being offered a recipe for the investigation but whether with the intention of leading or misleading, it was impossible to say. He was not deceived by Joseph's apparent calm or by his almost bantering manner. The old man had suffered sleepless hours; the skin was drawn more tightly over the bones of his skull, his eyes seemed more deeply set and he was even paler than when Wycliffe had first seen him.

Joseph lit a fresh cheroot. 'I gather you've given up smoking. I shall soon be old fashioned in that respect as in most others. Ernest gave it up four or five years back — drinking too in his case, except for the occasional sherry, but at seventy-five I feel that self denial is likely to prove an unrewarding investment.'

A marble mantel-clock which looked like a graveyard ornament chimed prettily. A quarter to twelve. Joseph waited for the sounds to die away. 'I should imagine your principal difficulty will be motive. It's hard to see how anyone in this house would have gained through the deaths of Jane and Alain Lemarque.'

The pale grey eyes watched him with speculative detachment but Wycliffe, bland, attentive, almost deferential, gave nothing away.

'Alain and Jane looked upon this as a second home while my wife was alive; they, with our three and Gerald, were like brothers and sisters. As you know, Gerald had a business relationship with Lemarque which, for a number of years, strengthened the bond. Of course things went very wrong there. Alain's business methods ran foul of the law and he ended up in jail.

Gerald had already broken with him but his political career was certainly not helped by the partnership. Even now it is a sensitive area.'

Joseph tapped the ash from his cheroot. 'Despite all that, it seems that Gerald was still prepared to put money into some scheme of Alain's. That shows how deeply they were attached. With Gerald's political prospects being what they are I think he was running a very considerable, perhaps a foolish risk of reviving old accusations and suspicions.'

Wycliffe thought: End of lesson. The old man had said his say; he would not embroider. He had made up his mind about Wycliffe's intelligence, its scope and limitations, and calculated the dose he judged to be sufficient. If the family had to suffer there was an obvious sacrificial candidate.

Well! Two could play at that game. Wycliffe got to his feet. 'Thank you for talking to me, Mr Bishop. Inspector Kersey will be asking you certain questions and inviting you to make a formal statement later.'

It was not what the old man had expected and he was immediately uneasy. He glanced at the mantel-clock. 'I usually allow myself a glass of sherry at about this time; why not stay and join me?'

But Wycliffe excused himself and went downstairs.

The house was silent except for the muffled tapping of the typewriter. Yet the impression of calm was an illusion. They were all there, bottled up: Joseph and his three offspring, his grandson, and Bateman. Bateman who was in the family but not of it. And the pearl in the oyster – the Lemarque girl. Six days ago Wycliffe had arrived, wondering about his reception, now they were all watching him with apprehension. Not that the fact gave him any satisfaction.

He pushed open the door of the dining-room. Kersey was seated on one side of the big table with Caroline opposite him. So Virginia had had her turn. Shaw, at one end, was filling that most ancient role of scribe as,

186

with slightly different materials, he might have done at the court of Sargon of Akkad, four millennia ago. Wycliffe wondered how long it would be before even low tech found its way into the legal labyrinth. By the window the typist was rattling out Virginia's statement which, later, she would be asked to sign.

Caroline glanced up as Wycliffe entered. She sat in one of the 'carvers' belonging to the dining suite, apparently relaxed, and somewhat slovenly in a woollen suit which seemed to cling in the wrong places.

'Did you see your husband shortly after lunch on Christmas Eve?'

'Yes, briefly, I was in the kitchen with my sister, washing up, when Gerald came in and said he was going for a walk. He had missed his morning walk and he likes to get in some exercise each day.'

'Do you happen to know at what time he returned from his walk?'

'No. The next time I saw him was between six and half-past when I went upstairs to put on a decent frock for the evening and he was in our bedroom changing into a suit.'

'You spent most of the afternoon in the kitchen?'

'Yes; getting ready for the evening.'

'Alone?'

'Most of the time. After we had finished washing up my sister went upstairs to do some cleaning but she came down again later.' Caroline glanced across at Wycliffe. 'The superintendent looked in at about half-past three to say that he was going out with Sergeant Curtis who had called to see him. My brother, Ernest, turned up shortly afterwards. We usually have a cup of tea around four. Ernest and I drank ours together in the kitchen then he took one up to father with a few biscuits . . . '

Wycliffe went over to the window and picked up the statement forms which had already been typed and were awaiting signature.

Virginia had said: 'Our housekeeper has the afternoons free and over Christmas there is a lot to do so my sister was working in the kitchen and I was upstairs doing some cleaning. I didn't come down again until nearly five, then I stayed with my sister in the kitchen getting things ready for the evening meal.'

Kersey was asking Caroline about the pistol.

'Of course I knew that my uncle had been presented with a pistol by the Maharajah of somewhere or other; it was part of the family lore, but it never occurred to me to wonder what had happened to it when he died and Aunt Stella moved in with us.'

'So you didn't know there was a pistol in the house?'

She made an impatient movement. 'I didn't know it or not know it; I simply never thought about it.'

Virginia had said: 'I knew the story about my uncle's pistol but I had no idea it was in the house.'

Kersey had finished with Caroline. 'Thank you Mrs Bateman.'

'Is that all?'

'For the present. We shall ask you to sign a statement later.'

She got up from her chair. Kersey looked after her as the door closed. 'She's a cool one. I wonder if she realizes how far she's helped to put her old man on the spot.'

Wycliffe was unsettled; he had an itch to be doing something but no clear idea what it should be. The interviews going on in the dining-room were an inquest into what had already happened; he was more concerned with what was likely to happen, what might be happening at this very moment. Where were the others? What was going on? What really troubled him was the possibility that the action might not be over.

If only he could smoke his pipe . . .

He left the dining-room and prowled about the hall like a suspicious dog sniffing out the corners. He found himself in the dark little passage behind the stairs which led to the kitchen. The kitchen door was ajar and he could hear voices. Ada was saying something in her sing-song brogue; then a man's voice. He pushed the door open.

Ada and Paul. Ada was at the sink, washing dishes, Paul was standing by her, listless, depressed. He must have come to her like that many times before, from infancy upwards. He looked around, startled, as Wycliffe came in; his eyes were red.

'Do you know where Francine is?'

The boy turned away. 'She's in her room, I think.' He was struggling to control his voice.

'Where is her room?'

Ada answered for him. 'Turn right at the top of the stairs and it's the last door on your left.'

'When did you begin to think that he might not be your natural father?'

She was sitting in a cane chair by the window of her room, looking out at the hillside swept by a curtain of rain. She wore jeans and a jumper of washed-out blue which suited her colouring. Her hair hung about her shoulders.

'At school last term we did a bit about human inheritance: blood groups, eye colour, hair colour, that sort of thing. I suppose that made me think. I brought home one of those do-it-yourself blood group cards and tried it on mother just out of curiosity. That was while he was still in prison.'

'And?' Like any good interviewer he tried to confine his questions to prompting.

'Well, when he came home I asked him if he knew what his blood group was and he said that when we lived in Richmond he'd been a donor. He was group O. Of course I knew then.'

'Did you say anything?'

'To mother, not to him.'

'What did she say?'

189

'She admitted it. She'd had a thing with Paul's father.' A helpless gesture. 'You saw the photographs in the album. Of course that was why she's been so concerned about Paul and me. Poor mother! She needn't have worried.'

She spoke slowly, in a low monotonous voice without emphasis or inflexion but it was the first time he had heard her give expression to any sentiment or admit to any sympathy.

'You've told Paul?'

'Only last night.'

'He seems very upset.'

A slight movement of the shoulders. 'He'll get over it. It will suit him better to be a brother when he gets used to it.'

'And your true father; have you said anything to him?'

'This morning. I only told him that I knew. He wanted to talk about it but I wouldn't.'

'You'll have to, sooner or later.'

'Perhaps.'

They were silent for a time; the only sounds came from water gurgling in a downpipe outside the window. It was raining harder and although it was still short of one o'clock the light was so poor that the girl was hardly more than a silhouette against the greyness outside.

She was the first to speak. 'What happens if you find out who killed my mother but you can't prove it?'

'I don't think that is very likely.'

'But it can happen?'

'Sometimes we think we know the identity of a criminal but we are unable to prove it to the satisfaction of a jury.'

'What then?'

'Either there is no prosecution or the prosecution fails.'

'And the criminal goes free?'

'A suspect is not a criminal until he is found guilty of a

crime.' Arid words but what else could he say? He was a policeman.

'I see.' After a pause she said: 'I suppose it depends on getting a good lawyer.'

He was concerned. 'I shouldn't think too much about it if I were you.'

She turned on him fiercely. 'You are talking about the man who killed my mother!'

He had never seen her so deeply moved and he was worried, but he hardly knew what to say. 'Your aunt will be back tomorrow.'

'I know.'

At shortly after one o'clock the interrogations were suspended and the police contingent went, in a body, to The Tributers. Afterwards Wycliffe and Kersey crossed over to the Incident Van where Fox was due with his photographs and a report on Lemarque's van.

One of the cubicles had been laid out with a display which could have been mistaken for a photographic exhibition and Fox was ready to expatiate but Wycliffe cut him short.

'At the moment we are only interested in the prints found inside the load compartment of the van.'

'Apart from Lemarque's, there were three sets, sir; two were several months old and probably belonged to the former owner, but the third set, on the inside door-handle, was quite fresh.'

Fox pointed to a blow-up of part of a thumb and three fingers of a right hand and there were still larger versions of the individual digits.

'No problem about identification if we get hold of a comparison set, sir.'

Kersey said: 'The man out walking his dog went past the van, our chap hiding inside was scared and got careless — is that the idea?'

Wycliffe was dour. 'That is the idea; let's hope it's the right one.'

CHAPTER TWELVE

It was after four o'clock and already almost dark when
the interviews were resumed in the dining-room at
Mynhager. Ada was first. Asked where she was on
Christmas Eve afternoon, she said she had spent it in
her room.

'What time did you leave your room?'

'I don't really know. Oh, yes I do, it must have been
about four because I saw Ernest taking in Mr Joseph's
tea.'

Bateman was next.

The cashmere cardigan had given place to a Harris
tweed jacket. Looking slightly pale but otherwise as
usual he sat opposite Kersey in the dining-room.
Wycliffe watched and wondered whether they would
achieve more than a fat file of statements.

'You gave an account of your movements on Christmas Eve to the chief superintendent.' Kersey turned to
Shaw: 'Read it please.'

Sergeant Shaw referred to his papers. 'Mr Bateman
said that he had visited the Lemarques at about 2.0 pm
on Christmas Eve afternoon and stayed only five
minutes. Afterwards he went for a walk which took him
to the hamlet of Busullow; he then returned to the main
road and came back through Morvah without meeting
anyone who remained in his memory.'

Kersey said: 'Would you like to amend that in any
way, sir?'

'No, that is what I did.'

'Can you say at what time you arrived back here?'

'Not exactly, but it would have been between half-past five and six.'

'So it was dark.'

'Oh, yes. Quite dark.'

'You know that Jane Lemarque was shot with a pistol which belonged to the late Major General Burnett-Price?'

'I have heard that, yes.'

'You knew about the pistol?'

'I knew that my uncle was given a pistol by a maharajah.'

'And that it was in the possession of your aunt?'

'I suppose I would have known that had I thought of it, but I didn't.'

Surprising the number of people who denied ever having thought about the pistol.

Bateman was gaining confidence; perhaps he was having an easier passage than he expected.

Kersey broached the possibility of blackmail but Bateman remained apparently unconcerned.

'You told Mr Wycliffe that you had not committed yourself to putting money into Lemarque's project. Is that correct?'

'Of course! How could I commit myself? I had no real idea what the project was.'

'Lemarque is supposed to have said that he could have taken you to jail with him; does that mean he was able to put pressure on you to support his scheme?'

A thin smile. 'To blackmail me, you mean. No, it does not. I've been the victim of gossip but I have never been vulnerable to blackmail by Lemarque or anyone else.'

Wycliffe was sitting at the end of the table furthest from the window, being as unobtrusive as possible but well aware that they were getting nowhere. Kersey, through no fault of his own, was fishing in dead water. What was needed was confrontation but a confrontation that achieves nothing is a self-inflicted wound.

However, it was a risk he had to take. He got up quietly and went out. In the hall, he knocked on the door of Ernest's study and went in.

Ernest was sitting at his table, the binocular microscope had been moved to one side and in front of him was an open book, the text interspersed with drawings of the wings of flies. But he was not working.

'I hope I'm not disturbing you.' The banal courtesy was ironic in the circumstances.

'Not at all.' In a tired voice. 'Is it my turn for the black chair?'

Wycliffe seemed at a loss. He stood by the table looking vaguely about him. He picked up a glass jar which held a number of specimen tubes in which maggots were stored in spirit.

'Are these the little tubes you carry about with you?'

'Yes, I use them for bringing back adult specimens as well as for storing larvae, but I don't suppose you came here to talk about flies.' Ernest's manner was subdued, almost resigned.

Wycliffe put the jar down. 'You must drive into Penzance almost every day, which way do you go?'

'There isn't much choice. I go from here to Treen then across the county through New Mill; it's only six or seven miles.'

Wycliffe was looking over the bookcase, packed with literature on entomology, from massive Victorian volumes to paper covered transactions and proceedings of the societies. Not a legal tome in sight.

'I suppose it's further if you go by way of Chysauster?'

'Chysauster?' Ernest's voice had suddenly sharpened but immediately he resumed a conversational tone. 'Yes, it's further and not a very good road. Why do you ask?'

'Will you drive me to Penzance?'

Ernest closed the book in front of him with slow deliberation. 'If you wish. In the morning, perhaps?'

'Now.'

'If you say so.' Ernest displayed the absorbed concentration of a man picking his way through a minefield.

Wycliffe led the way out into the hall. He opened the door of the dining-room and spoke to Kersey. 'Mr Bishop is going to drive me to Penzance and I would like you and Mr Bateman to come with us.'

Bateman turned in his chair. 'May I ask the purpose of this excursion?'

'I want to clear up certain points which may have a bearing on this investigation.' Deliberately meaningless and as pompous. Bateman, about to protest, thought better of it.

A few minutes later the four men, wearing raincoats, trooped out into the courtyard. It was quite dark except for the light from the house, and rain blew in from the sea. The watcher in the Panda car got out and approached Kersey.

Wycliffe said: 'Borrow his torch.'

Ernest reversed his car out of the old coach house and the three of them climbed in. Wycliffe insisted on Bateman travelling in front with Ernest.

At a sedate speed they covered the seven miles to Penzance almost in silence. Once Bateman said: 'This strikes me as some kind of charade! I hope it has some purpose.'

There was no response. As they reached the railway station on the outskirts of the town Ernest asked where he should take them.

'Drive along the waterfront and the promenade and stop by the Royal Hotel.'

There were few people about; Mounts Bay was a void, with the lights of Newlyn and Mousehole twinkling through the rain. Ernest drove the length of the promenade, negotiated the roundabout, and returned to pull up outside the Royal Hotel. When he cut the engine they could hear the waves breaking along the shore.

'Well, do we get out?' From Bateman.

'No, we go back by a different route.'

In a voice that was scarcely recognizable as his own, Ernest asked: 'What route is that?'

Wycliffe said: 'On Easter Saturday 1979 you both attended a dinner at this hotel. Lemarque was a guest. Do you remember the occasion?'

A barely audible affirmative from Ernest.

Bateman said: 'I told you I was the guest speaker.'

'You drove home together?'

'Naturally, but I can't see how it can have any possible connection with the crimes you are supposed to be investigating and I protest most strongly against this . . . this melodrama!'

'You are under no obligation to co-operate; perhaps you would prefer more formal questioning at the police station?'

'You are threatening me, Chief Superintendent.'

'No sir. I am offering you an alternative. So the three of you drove home together. In this car?'

'Yes.'

'Mr Bishop, were you driving on that occasion?'

A police prowl car cruised along the promenade, slowed suspiciously as it drew level with them, then continued on its way.

Ernest said: 'I can't remember who was driving.'

'Mr Bateman?'

'To the best of my recollection, it was Lemarque.'

'And Lemarque is dead. At any rate you set out from here at about midnight. It was raining, as it is tonight. All I am asking is that we reconstruct your journey home. Shall we start?'

Ernest switched on the engine and they moved off, back along the promenade and the wharf, past the railway station, then they left the coast road and began the steady climb to the central moorland. As they were approaching the first fork Wycliffe said: 'Instead of turning off left, keep on this road.'

Ernest obeyed without comment but Bateman was

truculent: 'You realize, I suppose, that we are now on our way to St Ives?'

The road climbed steeply between rows of cottages which soon gave place to hedges. Phantom streaks of rain gleamed in the headlights and the screen wipers beat with the regularity of a metronome. Wycliffe tried to convince himself that he was not organizing a fiasco. The greenish light from the dashboard lit up the faces of the two men in front, obliquely and in profile. Kersey sat, hunched in his corner, so still that he could have been asleep.

'Turn left at Badger's Cross and that will bring us back eventually to the road home.'

'Which we need not have left as far as I can see.' Bateman again.

At Badger's Cross Ernest turned off into a lane which ran between high hedges; it was undulating and sinuous. From time to time the headlights picked out a farm gate, or a stile, and once or twice they saw the lights of a house. Wycliffe had in his mind an accurate picture of the area for, apart from studying the map, he had driven along the road in the small hours of the morning.

'On the night of your dinner, at about midnight, a girl was walking home along this road. She had been visiting a friend in the house now coming up on our right and she lived about a mile further on. She was nineteen, home on vacation from a teacher training college.'

Ernest was driving even more slowly now; the old Rover revved away, mostly in second gear and the hedges crept by with majestic slowness.

A road sign, caught and held in the headlights, read: 'Chysauster: Ancient Village'. The remnants of a cluster of iron-age huts lay two or three fields away, up on their right; a bleak place.

'The girl was killed in a hit-and-run and the police were convinced they were looking for a drunken driver but they never found him; torrential rain later that night had washed away any clues there might have been.

'The girl's father searched the road between the two houses but failed to find her and called in the police. By that time it was raining heavily and they were working under difficulties but they found her at last, dead. She had been dragged off the road into a ditch. It was then half-past three in the morning.'

Wycliffe was talking into a wall of silence. Once Bateman turned abruptly in his seat as though to say something but he did not speak.

The headlights shone on a house straight ahead which seemed to block the way. Ernest negotiated a ninety-degree turn at snail's pace then stalled the engine as he tried to accelerate. 'I'm not going on with this!' But there was more of despair than defiance in his voice.

'Will you drive, Mr Bateman?'

'Certainly not!'

'Then Mr Kersey . . .'

Without a word Kersey got out and went round the car to take Ernest's place at the wheel. Ernest climbed into the back with Wycliffe. 'I'm sorry . . .'

Wycliffe said to Kersey: 'About a quarter-of-a-mile; I'll tell you when to stop.'

Kersey restarted the engine and they cruised down a gentle slope, past another little house with outbuildings.

'At the bottom.'

Kersey pulled off the road on to a patch of rough grass and brought the car to a halt. When he cut the engine the silence was complete.

'The pathologist reported that the girl had suffered a compound fracture of the left femur along with other less serious injuries, none of them likely to prove fatal in ordinary circumstances. The compound fracture was complicated by her being moved off the road into the ditch but the immediate cause of death was loss of blood. She bled to death and, according to the pathologist, it would have taken about three hours.'

The windows were beginning to steam up and Wycliffe wound down the one on his side, letting in the moist night air and the fresh but slightly acrid smell of the moor.

'This is the place where it happened. The girl lived in a little house at the top of the next slope. You can see the light.'

Although the evening was not cold Wycliffe shivered. Suddenly in a harsh voice he said: 'Get out and see for yourselves where she died!'

They trooped out like tourists on their way to inspect some curiosity *en route*. They crossed the road, Kersey played his torch on the ground and lit up the ditch which was overhung by gorse and brambles.

Wycliffe's voice came, dry and unrelenting. 'She was walking on the right hand side of the road. There was plenty of room for any vehicle to pass.'

They stood there, a disconsolate group with the quiet rain sifting out of the darkness.

'All they found here was a few fragments of broken glass – very thin glass, perhaps a broken specimen tube. It meant nothing to the police at the time.'

Bateman had been silent for a while, now in a more conciliatory tone, he said: 'Of course we knew of this tragedy, Mr Wycliffe, everyone did in this part of the county at least, but I cannot see—'

'Shut up!' Wycliffe's voice, vicious with suppressed anger, silenced the politician as if a switch had been thrown. They stood there a little longer in the moist darkness then, wearily, Wycliffe said: 'Let's get back.'

Kersey took the wheel and they drove up the slope, past the house where the girl had lived, then down the other side to join their road back just beyond New Mill. Another fifteen minutes and they were pulling into the courtyard at Mynhager. Not a word had been spoken on the way.

Caroline was in the hall where a uniformed constable tried hard to be invisible. She tackled her husband: 'What the hell is happening?'

Bateman snapped: 'I've no idea!'

'Those cretins in there wouldn't tell me anything.'

Wycliffe ignored her and turned to the two men. 'I want to talk to you in the dining-room, one at a time; you first, Mr Bishop. Mr Bateman will remain with the constable.'

In the dining-room Ernest occupied the chair. Shaw was in his place at the end of the big table and the typist had moved away from the window into a better light. Wycliffe did not sit down but stood near Ernest's chair. His voice was hard, his manner abrasive.

'Jane Lemarque was shot with a pistol taken from your aunt's room and returned there without her knowledge. So the killer is a member of this household; one of the family.'

Ernest said nothing; he sat, his soft white hands clasped tightly together, on the table in front of him.

'Lemarque was also shot but we have no evidence concerning the weapon though I think defence counsel would have difficulty in separating the two crimes.'

Ernest removed his spectacles and began to polish them.

'The problem was motive; neither Bateman's possible involvement in the Lemarque frauds nor the question of Francine's parentage, both hinted at by your father, seemed to stand up. It was only in following up the curious matter of Lemarque's press cutting, reporting your dinner, that I came upon the hit-and-run affair and finally linked the two. Three professional men on their way home after a night out. The driver was so drunk that he missed his way on a familiar road, and a girl was knocked down, injured, and pushed into a ditch to die.'

There was a long silence. Wycliffe was oppressed by the contemptible shabbiness he had uncovered, by a spectacle of self-interest carried to the length of murder so that three lives were sacrificed to secure the personal ambition of a politician and the comfortable humdrum existence of a small-town lawyer.

Ernest broke the silence at last; in a low voice he said: 'We thought she was dead. Lemarque was quite positive.' He coughed, then spoke more strongly. 'He said he was absolutely certain and he was the only one who touched her. Otherwise . . . '

Wycliffe drew a deep breath like a sigh, then in a voice that was almost coaxing he said: 'Lemarque was not driving that night, was he?'

There was an interval. Shaw and the typist, roused out of their professional apathy, were hanging on Ernest's words. 'I was.'

Wycliffe turned to Shaw. 'Ask Mr Bateman to join us please.'

Ernest sat motionless, staring straight in front of him, his features devoid of any expression.

Bateman came in, alert, suspicious, metaphorically sniffing the air. Wycliffe pointed to a chair next to Ernest. 'Please sit down,' and went on at once: 'We now know that Mr Bishop was driving his car when the accident involving the girl occurred.'

Bateman looked at Ernest, then at Wycliffe, hoping for a lead but found none. 'Is this some kind of trap?'

'Ask Mr Bishop.'

In a flat voice Ernest said: 'I told him. I've lived with this for five years and, God knows, that is long enough.'

It was impossible to interpret Bateman's expression but he must have been struggling desperately to adjust and adapt, finally he seemed to resign himself: 'Then we shall have to pay for our folly. All I can say is that if I had suspected for a moment that the girl was not dead I would have summoned assistance whatever the consequences. As it was, I allowed myself to be persuaded. Believing that nothing could be done for her I admit that I did consider the possible consequences of making a report. Ernest's whole career and way of life would have been irreparably damaged and, though I was only a passenger in the car, I should have suffered politically.

My decision was highly improper but, in the circumstances, I think understandable.'

A worthy extempore performance.

Wycliffe was staring intently at Bateman. His face gave nothing away but under his gaze Bateman became increasingly restless. He began to tap on the table with the fingers of his right hand, a tension reflex which had often irritated his colleagues in the House.

'I can well understand: a country-town lawyer and an ambitious politician. I doubt if even clergymen are so vulnerable.' Wycliffe was scathing. 'After you had failed to call assistance at the time of the accident and even more so when it became known that the girl had not died until three hours after she had been dragged into a ditch, you both knew without a shadow of a doubt that the truth would ruin you. As a businessman and an entrepreneur Lemarque might have scraped by, but a lawyer, and a politician with a taste for office . . . ' He spoke directly to Bateman: 'You must have realized too that the business was so unsavoury that even those people who will sometimes provide a niche for a discredited politician would have found you untouchable.'

Bateman's fingers were working overtime, tapping out a monotonous rhythm. 'Will you tell me where all this is leading?'

'To the point that you were wide open to blackmail and Lemarque was quick to take advantage of the fact when he came out of jail. "Five years ago", he said, "we were all three of us in the same boat or should I say car? Not any more! I no longer belong to the club." You remember Lemarque on the telephone? I can see that you do. From that point onwards your political career was going to be expensive. No doubt Ernest's turn would come but you were to be first in line.'

Ernest sat quite motionless, staring down at the table top.

'But Lemarque had underestimated you and that mistake cost him and his wife their lives.

202

'You weren't your brother-in-law, he would have bought his peace of mind. Or tried to.'

Bateman had come to a decision. 'I have nothing more to say. I am in your hands for the moment, but I warn you that I shall exercise all my rights under the law.'

'What you say is noted. The constable in the hall will go with you to your room and you will point out to him the clothing you were wearing on Christmas Eve afternoon. This will be checked and sent for forensic examination. Later you will be escorted to the Divisional police station where your fingerprints will be taken for comparison with prints found inside Lemarque's van. You will be given the opportunity to make statements in respect of the hit-and-run accident and the unlawful killings of Alain and Jane Lemarque.'

To his surprise Bateman raised no objection; he would make no more difficulties and answer no more questions until he was in the hands of his lawyer. Wycliffe signed to Kersey who escorted him into the hall.

Wycliffe was left in the dining-room with Ernest, Sergeant Shaw, and the young typist. They heard voices, footsteps on the stairs, then nothing.

Ernest had scarcely moved, he sat staring at his hands, clasped together on the table top. In a tired voice he asked: 'What happens to me?'

'You will be taken to the police station and given the opportunity of making a statement in connection with the hit-and-run accident. You will be asked further questions in connection with the deaths of Lemarque and his wife.'

The minutes dragged by, the silence broken only by the sporadic rattle of the typewriter. Wycliffe wondered what was happening to the others. Were they gathered together, speculating on the turn things had taken or were they each hiding in their separate cells? And of the future: what would happen to Francine? Would she go

203

back with her aunt to a new and different world? Wycliffe felt sure she would not; far more likely that she would join the Mynhager ménage where life would go on much as before free of intrusions by the alien Bateman.

In rapid succession three shots echoed through the old house as through a cavern. Wycliffe made for the door, crossed the hall, and bounded up the stairs. On the first landing Kersey was bending over Bateman who lay in a great pool of blood; the uniformed constable was standing by, dazed, still holding a plastic bag full of clothing.

In a voice scarcely recognizable, Kersey said: 'Dead! Shot through the neck and chest. I saw her standing on the landing when they went up to his room but the gun was hidden ... Then, as they came back along the corridor to the top of the stairs, she fired ...'

Wycliffe heard Shaw preventing the family from coming up; mercifully it seemed that they were all downstairs. Francine was standing just a few feet from the dead man, the gun still in her hand, held limply at her side.

'Give it to me.'

She did so without a word.

Wycliffe was in the Incident Van; rain drummed on the roof. Potter was at the duty desk; it was almost midnight. A car drew up outside, a door slammed and a minute or so later Kersey came in.

'Well?'

'I've handed her over. A W.P.C. is looking after her and she seems perfectly calm. She insisted on taking her black doll with her.'

For a long time the two men sat opposite each other in silence. Wycliffe was the first to speak.

'I feel responsible. It never occurred to me that she had taken Lemarque's gun with her when she left home, yet from her point of view it was an obvious precaution.'

204

'On the principle of keeping matches away from children.'

'Yes, you could put it like that. She cross questioned me about what would happen if we couldn't prove our case and I still didn't see . . .'

Kersey said: 'She wasn't prepared to leave anything to chance.'

THE END

WYCLIFFE AND THE DEAD FLAUTIST
by W.J. Burley

On the secluded estate of Lord and Lady Bottrel, the body of amateur flautist Tony Mills was found, shot by his own gun – apparently suicide. But a closer examination revealed some rather sinister inconsistencies and Chief Superintendent Wycliffe was called in.

As he began to unravel the last days of the dead man, another mystery was revealed – the disappearance of Lizzie Biddick, pretty young maid at the Bottrel ancestral home. Gradually bitter family feuds and secret illicit relationships were uncovered, and then another body was found, shattering for ever the pastoral peace of the Cornish estate.

0 552 14264 6

WYCLIFFE AND THE TANGLED WEB
by W.J. Burley

Hilda Clemo, bright, beautiful, still at school, dropped the bombshell of her pregnancy to her family and boyfriend – and then vanished from her Cornish village that same summer afternoon. As fears for her safety grew, Chief Superintendent Wycliffe was brought in to search the fields and cliffs and question the Clemo family – a weird, feuding clan whose kinship and hatreds covered some unpleasant secrets.

One of the secrets finally led to the discovery of a body – but not the body of Hilda Clemo. By the time Hilda's corpse was found, Wycliffe had a welter of mysteries to solve, not least the true character of the precocious murdered schoolgirl.

0 552 14268 9

WYCLIFFE AND THE LAST RITES
by W.J. Burley

Michael Jordan, vicar of Moresk, felt a tremor of disquiet even before he opened the door of his sixteenth-century church. There was the noise – a sustained chord of jarring notes from the organ – and the fact that the padlock was missing from the doors. Inside was a hideous violation of the chancel – the body of Jessica Dobell, partially unclothed and with her skull smashed in.

At first the village thought is must be the work of a Satanist cult, but when Superintendent Wycliffe arrived he didn't agree. There was an air of violent hatred prevalent in the village, and not all of it was directed towards the dead woman.

When the second murder occurred, Wycliffe knew he had to act quickly – but even though he thought he knew who the killer was, how could he prove it?

0 552 14265 4

WYCLIFFE AND HOW TO KILL A CAT
by W.J. Burley

The girl was slim and young, with auburn hair splayed out on the pillow. Wycliffe almost believed her asleep rather than dead – until he saw her face. Although death was by strangulation, someone had smashed her face in after she was dead. She lay in a sordid room in a seedy hotel down by the docks, but her luggage, her clothes, and her make-up all indicated she was more expensive and classier than her surroundings.

Superintendent Wycliffe was officially on holiday, but the case fascinated him and he had to find out who she was, why she was lying naked in a shabby hotel room, why she had a thousand pounds hidden under some clothing, and above all, why she had been 'murdered' twice.

As he began to investigate, he found there was too much of everything about the case – too many suspects, too many motives, and too many lies.

0 552 14117 8

A SELECTED LIST OF CRIME NOVELS
AVAILABLE FROM CORGI BOOKS

☐	13232 2	WYCLIFFE AND THE BEALES	*W.J. Burley*	£3.99
☐	14264 6	WYCLIFFE AND THE DEAD FLAUTIST	*W.J. Burley*	£3.99
☐	14221 2	WYCLIFFE AND THE DUNES MYSTERY	*W.J. Burley*	£4.99
☐	14268 9	WYCLIFFE AND THE TANGLED WEB	*W.J. Burley*	£3.99
☐	14109 7	WYCLIFFE AND THE CYCLE OF DEATH	*W.J. Burley*	£4.99
☐	13689 1	WYCLIFFE AND DEATH IN STANLEY STREET	*W.J. Burley*	£3.99
☐	14267 0	WYCLIFFE AND THE FOUR JACKS	*W.J. Burley*	£3.99
☐	14266 2	WYCLIFFE AND THE SCAPEGOAT	*W.J. Burley*	£3.99
☐	12805 8	WYCLIFFE AND THE SCHOOLGIRLS	*W.J. Burley*	£3.99
☐	14269 7	WYCLIFFE'S WILD-GOOSE CHASE	*W.J. Burley*	£4.99
☐	13436 8	WYCLIFFE AND THE WINSOR BLUE	*W.J. Burley*	£3.99
☐	13433 3	WYCLIFFE IN PAUL'S COURT	*W.J. Burley*	£4.99
☐	12804 X	WYCLIFFE AND THE PEA-GREEN BOAT	*W.J. Burley*	£3.99
☐	14265 4	WYCLIFFE AND THE LAST RITES	*W.J. Burley*	£4.99
☐	14117 8	WYCLIFFE AND HOW TO KILL A CAT	*W.J. Burley*	£3.99
☐	14115 1	WYCLIFFE AND THE GUILT EDGED ALIBI	*W.J. Burley*	£4.99
☐	14205 0	WYCLIFFE AND THE THREE-TOED PUSSY	*W.J. Burley*	£4.99
☐	14116 X	WYCLIFFE AND DEATH IN A SALUBRIOUS PLACE	*W.J. Burley*	£3.99
☐	14437 1	WYCLIFFE AND THE HOUSE OF FEAR	*W.J. Burley*	£4.99
☐	14043 0	SHADOW PLAY	*Frances Fyfield*	£4.99
☐	14174 7	PERFECTLY PURE AND GOOD	*Frances Fyfield*	£4.99
☐	14295 6	A CLEAR CONSCIENCE	*Frances Fyfield*	£4.99
☐	14223 9	BORROWED TIME	*Robert Goddard*	£5.99
☐	13840 1	CLOSED CIRCLE	*Robert Goddard*	£5.99
☐	13839 8	HAND IN GLOVE	*Robert Goddard*	£5.99
☐	14555 6	A TOUCH OF FROST	*R.D. Wingfield*	£4.99
☐	13981 5	FROST AT CHRISTMAS	*R.D. Wingfield*	£5.99
☐	14558 0	NIGHT FROST	*R.D. Wingfield*	£5.99
☐	14409 6	HARD FROST	*R.D. Wingfield*	£5.99

All Transworld titles are available by post from:

Book Service By Post, P.O. Box 29, Douglas, Isle of Man IM99 1BQ

Credit cards accepted. Please telephone 01624 675137,
fax 01624 670923, Internet http://www.bookpost.co.uk
or e-mail: bookshop@enterprise.net for details.

Free postage and packing in the UK. Overseas customers: allow
£1 per book (paperbacks) and £3 per book (hardbacks).